RETURN TO EDEN

THE WILDERNESS YEARS

Elegy

Grosvenor House
Publishing Limited

This book is published by
Grosvenor House Publishing Ltd
Link House
140 The Broadway, Tolworth, Surrey, KT6 7HT.
www.grosvenorhousepublishing.co.uk

A CIP record for this book
is available from the British Library

ISBN 978-1-83975-920-8

To
LYNNE

PROLOGUE

England in the time of his boyhood was a cold and colourless country.

They had seen to that, the Autumn Men.

They who had been lifted high. The old men of his country and other countries, who in the autumn of their years, reflecting on the unfulfilled promise of their youth, and their failures as yet unredeemed, feeling as any old man adrift alone on a small boat, sails broken, oars lost, swept hopelessly onward towards the deafening roar of the approaching weir, might feel, decided that too few had sweetly and honourably been called.

So call out the young men, wide-eyed and brave of heart, to don uniform, bid sweethearts farewell and forfeit their future.

And murder in the name of God.

Until they, too, are harvested 'neath the Autumn Men's sickle.

And the lark song is stilled as passing bells are heard anew.

No longer could the innocent look to the heavens for salvation, but only look on in horror as the devil poured the contents of hell over them.

And so it was, and so it remained until Satan, who had found refuge in the hearts of too many, was cast out and the women had cried, 'Enough!'

And on countless memorials in towns and villages across the cold and colourless country, new names were added to the old, and memorials once again were baptised with tears of the innocent for the innocent. And in the great city, as the weak winter sunshine filters through the mists of an early November morning, the Autumn Men in their black coats and polished shoes still stand, shameless, in solemn line to bow their heads and lay poppy-lit wreaths, mankind's apology to its youth.

This, then, was the wasteland of his boyhood. One from which he would spend the rest of his life trying to escape.

CHAPTER ONE

He was cold. He hated the cold. He stood shivering at the entrance to the garden centre, anxiously peering out over the raised artificial pond where fat, sulky, barbed carp swam aimlessly through grey silky water. He was hoping to catch a glimpse of her car. He thrust his gloved hands deep into his overcoat pockets and silently stamped his feet, a pantomimic gesture designed as much to relieve his mounting frustration as any serious attempt to facilitate circulation.

He was waiting for his daughter, Catherine. She was late. She was always late. Any simmering anger he may have felt, however, was tempered as he recalled, with almost unbearable pain, how increasingly sad and dissolute her life had been, and the unwitting role he had played in it, being too far away when she needed him the most. A faraway place where he had fought long battles with his demons and the voices and the faces of his past, and from where he believed he had emerged triumphant.

Catherine's mother, Suzanne, who had also been absent for long periods, had been a beautiful and talented artist. She had long ago retreated into the sanctuary of a world which allowed entry to no-one, including her daughter, but not before being driven blindly to that point where she felt even her sanity to be under threat, when her heart and spirit were broken as she realised she was losing him. She had committed wanton acts of cruelty that would almost destroy her and those she professed to love, acts against morality, decency, her religion, and finally, her God.

And there, in that soulless sanctuary, she remained, loveless.

Catherine was an only child, shy and sensitive, who had grown up under the strict supervision of a series of governesses in a series of lonely households. She had attended the finest boarding schools and the best finishing school. She was a stranger to cold, hunger, want… and love.

Her schooling complete – having learnt everything about nothing that mattered, and nothing about everything that did – she found herself alone in a hostile world. At her mother's insistence and with her mother's money, she commenced a peripatetic existence, moving from one great European city to another. Sometimes, she would stay with friends of her mother in sunlit country houses, where on high summer days she would hide away with her shyness in their great gardens, with their clipped topiary, avenues of cascading laburnum, rose-ladened pergolas, and Roman statues. There, she would sit lost in thought on the child's swing that hung from the outstretched arm of a giant cedar. Other times, she would stay in crumbling palaces by the edge of Venetian canals, where on late autumnal days she would hide away with her shyness in the ghostly grey mists that rose from the canals and settled like tears on the dying buildings and sighing bridges. There, she would sit lost in thought among the decaying splendour of some great gothic church, surrounded by rare and beautiful objects that no-one seemed to see or value.

All around her people were relaxed, humorous, charming. In the evening, candlelit dinners would be held, where the gifted and the beautiful would be called to the table to entertain their fellow guests with light-hearted conversation, effortless wit, and a seemingly endless supply of outrageous anecdotes – always with a glass in their hand, and a bottle to refresh it in close attendance.

Like so many before her, she believed alcohol could be the answer to all her ills. And for a while it was; the sudden surge of wellbeing and the exhilaration acted on her like morphine – instant pain relief.

And like so many before her, she too quickly realised that alcohol created just an illusion, leaving only the embarrassment of what she had said and the shame of what she had done.

She also learnt that such illusions and such consequences would prove to be far more preferable to the ice-cold of reality and the stomach-churning terror of facing another day without it.

When at last she tired of the beautiful people – or, more often than not, when they tired of her – she would move from hotel to hotel, carrying everything she needed in a small suitcase, following the sun, following the seasons. An empty, endless journey to nowhere. Unfulfilled, lacking any purpose or sense of direction, she was drowning in the meaninglessness of her life.

Like so many before her, she concluded that love would be the answer. So she devoted herself to finding and holding onto that which she had never known. She chased love blindly, to satiate a need deep inside her that she herself could not explain. But in doing so, she demanded more than anyone could give, and the intensity of her needs served only to instil fear in those who, given time, may have grown to love her. Instead, desperate after too many heart breaks and too many rejections, she gave herself away too easily, too cheaply, to anyone who showed her a kindness. One by one, they deserted her, leaving only those who, seeking to benefit from her desperation, abused, humiliated, and betrayed her.

And like so many before her, she learnt that, despite the passage of time, the wounds of betrayal never heal.

Reluctantly, nursing her broken heart and sacrificing what little pride she had left, she returned to England and the home of the stranger she called Mother. But her mother, and perhaps she herself, had lived alone for too long; neither could offer what the other needed. Never had she felt more distant from her mother, nor more alone, than during that time of chill they spent together. Left with too much time to think, she found no solace, no peace, no contentment. Feeling increasingly isolated, she succumbed to despair, believing – for she had never been told otherwise – that she was unlovely and unloved. Wearied by the empty days of nothingness and the nights of never-ending darkness, and dulled by drink, she would lie on her bed calling out for her father, recalling that neither he nor her mother had ever held her close, or kissed her, or told her they loved her.

A form of respite that both looked forward to came each weekend when her mother packed her palettes and her easel into her car, and they drove to her cottage in the country. The cottage had been purchased with the proceeds of what she referred to as 'her limelight days', when she had sought out, gained, and exploited fame. Now, she sought only the shadows.

Her age-weathered, grey-golden stone cottage lay isolated in the fold of a hill at the bottom of a high-hedged lane, and faced out onto undulating pastureland where Jacob sheep roamed restlessly in still fields. Shepherd-less.

Entrance was gained through an ancient, heavy black oak door, above which, carved into the oak lintel, was the date 1594 and the name TEMBANI'. The door led into a large, gloomy room that was bathed in thin, weak, grey light. and was dominated by a massive inglenook fireplace. The floor was stone-flagged, and the walls covered with dark oak panelling. The ceiling beams throughout were of oak that had been felled in Shakespeare's time. A narrow, winding, stone staircase hugged one wall as it rose to two tiny bedrooms, each with a skylight cut through the thatch. It was here, when sleep failed to find her, that Suzanne would gaze at the ever-changing starlit, moonlit sky.

The cottage was sparse and bleak. No pictures hung from the panelled walls; no carpets warmed the floors. An aged, black Chesterfield, cracked and faded, faced the fireplace. On one side stood a single lamp on a table; on the other, a gramophone.

The rectangular-shaped back garden was reached through a whitewashed, spartan kitchen where a solitary cold-water tap, jutting out from the wall beneath the mullion window, dripped into a deep stone sink.

Climbing roses, clematis, and rambling honeysuckle clung to the high-sided dry-stone walls that formed the boundary on either side of the garden. Sun-seeking wild flowers and emeralds of moss grew between the stones. A thick trunked wisteria covered the whole of the back wall of the cottage, its spreading branches overhanging the windows, clinging to and twisting through the wire mesh that supported the thatch. A meandering, crazy paving path sloped gently down to a silver stream at the bottom of the garden that was shaded by tall silver birch and low leaning rowan, and whose waters ran icy cold regardless of the season. On either side of the path, the borders were graced with a multitude of perennial shrubs of varying height, textures, and hues, which died each autumn and were resurrected each spring.

A round, white painted table and iron chair stood in isolation on a small patio that was dressed with wooden tubs and terracotta pots of salmon-pink pelargonium.

The cottage itself was surrounded by farmland, unchanged in centuries. Immediately beyond the stream were fields of grassland, where generations of sheep had grazed, and wild flowers flourished. Criss-crossed by hedgerows and winding lanes, the fields were reached through five-bar gates and styles. Stretching far into the distance, where the land met the sky, were endless swathes of poppy-studded fields of barley and corn. Birdsong echoed from the hedgerows. On late summer evenings, she would be out picking blackberries in the narrow lanes, inking her fingers and her lips and her blouse. Alerted by the approaching clip-clopping of a pair of towering Shire horses, Sunday best-dressed in polished leather harness and shiny brasses, she would be forced to back into the brambles, her basket pressed against her chest as they passed her by, drawing their high sided cart of freshly harvested corn.

It was to here, her cottage, that she would return time after time, escaping unkindness, fleeing from the outside world with its brutality and its ugliness. It was here, and only here, that she found the peace and the contentment she so desperately sought.

A distant church clock chimed nine. Musically, soft rain began to fall, pitter-pattering onto the pond and bowing the heads of the late flowering daffodils. The carp retreated to the depths. Although it was early spring, and the buds on the chestnut trees bordering the car park were beginning to unfold, to him it was still bitterly cold. The pewter sky seemed to weigh even more heavily on him than usual. He instinctively knew there was nothing to be overly concerned about regarding his daughter's immediate welfare, no harm would come to her this day. The gift he had long possessed assured him of that – a gift confirmed by his grandmother at a fateful meeting when he was just a boy of 15; a gift that had never failed him.

He knew little of his grandmother; few did. Those who knew the least gossiped the most. The raven blackness of her hair, her olive-shaped eyes, and the darkness of her skin, suggested foreign ancestry. It was said she had married – if in fact she had married – at the age of 12, and given birth to ten children, seven of whom had survived. No-one knew how old she was. It was common knowledge that she was rich, but no-one knew how rich or how she had come by her wealth. All of her children loathed and feared her. All of their spouses were terrified of her and the viciousness of her tongue. She had demanded much of her children, and all had failed her. She considered them all to be weak and idle. All left home at the first opportunity; neither they nor she ever regretting the decision. Her grandchildren she disowned. Surprisingly, Jackie knew even less of his own parents, save that his father had defied the will of his mother – his grandmother – and married the 16-year-old daughter of a German family who had arrived in England just before the war.

Having waited for too long in the cold, he decided to return to the warmth of the cafeteria inside the garden centre, which would be opening by now, and where, without prompting, he would be given tea and his morning newspapers.

When events had dictated that he return from his beloved Mediterranean farmhouse, it was to here, this little rural market town by the sea, that he had reluctantly and painfully decided to settle, to be close to his daughter and Suzanne. Bringing nothing more than indifference to the task in hand, he had decided to live in an upmarket and modern apartment with sea views, in an affluent area. And he had come to bitterly regret his decision. However, he had found a form of refuge in the garden centre, and after a time came to love and look forward to his visits. He would never himself use the word 'love', recalling that his grandmother had instilled in him the belief that it was the most debased word in the English language, and on too many occasions it had been proven to him that she was correct.

Eventually, after careful consideration, he convinced himself that it would be prudent to purchase, very discreetly, a not insubstantial share in the business. Not because he wished to be involved in its day-to-day operation, he did not, but so that he would have somewhere to go every day where he would find the warmth and colour and hope that he had left behind.

The staff knew him and knew not to disturb him, aware that he intensely disliked over-familiarisation. As the months slowly passed, however, something approaching affection had grown in him as he observed that they were a friendly, helpful, and good-natured family of friends, who enjoyed and took pride and pleasure in their work. They were a dignified people, apt to keep their personal lives private, and not weigh others down with their burdens.

He had a little office in a recess next to the kitchen entrance. To protect his privacy, he could look out from a small window into the cafeteria and garden centre, but no-one was able to look in. From this vantage point he was able to engage in the activity that had long fascinated him – the simple act of observing people, and from their demeanour and actions speculate about them and the lives they led. There was nothing sinister in this activity; he simply wanted to understand why they were so different to him. From the moment he first began to think, he had been able to feel this difference. Because of what he was, because of the way he looked, because of what he had become, he had never been able to experience anything like a normal relationship with his fellows. They felt awkward and sometimes threatened in his presence, and he had never found a way of preventing this. In fact, too often in later life he had encouraged it. However, in a peculiar way he believed it was this difference, this separation, that allowed him to observe them so intensely in such a detached manner.

As a friendless man, long comfortable in his aloneness, it was surprising the warmth he felt towards that particular breed of customer who regularly visited the garden centre, almost as if, he thought, an act of reaffirmation of life itself. Those who may only have a window box or hanging baskets either side of the door, but had an imagination that no boundaries could contain. They, too, could have a dream, he believed; a dream of boundless horizons. To create a magnificent garden of their own perhaps, from nothing more than a barren landscape. Or an orchard of old and rare English varieties mostly long forgotten, with white and pink confetti showers of blossom in the spring, and red and green and russet apples in the autumn. Or, he imagined, they might dream of creating a great lake, bordered by bulrushes concealing nests of coot chicks, replenished by willows weeping at its edge. Or perhaps, they secretly wished to create a garden of their childhood memories, with rainbows of lupins, beehives of foxgloves, tepees of hanging beans, and ripening pods of pick-me peas, where they could sit on warm summer evenings – a sanctuary from the deafening sounds of an alien world.

Those, who for some obscure reason he most admired, however, were the 'seeds-men'. They would gather before the seed stands, those tumbling waterfalls of colour, studying each packet in turn, as if for the first time, carefully reading the instructions that they themselves could have written, before finally choosing old and trusted friends. These were the people who, he imagined, on deep and dark December evenings would sit on three-legged stools in moonlit, stove-warmed glasshouses, beside wooden benches strewn with clay pots of all shapes and sizes. Here, they would open the packets as reverently as a priest would open a Bible, handle the seeds as if they were diamonds, and delight in the as yet unfulfilled promise they offered.

The seeds would be set and nurtured through the long cold days of winter. Night after night they would be visited, receiving encouraging words if responding well, or gently chastised if reluctant to make an appearance. The days would lengthen and they would grow stronger. Refusing to be hurried by the fools-gold warmth of deceitful May, the seeds-men, Job patient, would wait until the first week of June, and in a flurry of activity release them into their gardens and watch in wonder throughout the summer days as they grew and flourished and bloomed. Then, in the misty dying days of autumn, they would produce their own seeds to be gathered in, and the mysterious cycle of life would begin anew.

This, then, was how he imagined the lives of these people. These were the dreams he hoped they dreamed.

Perhaps, in reality, it was simply that this was how he wished his own life could have been.

Though now approaching his mid-fifties, he was still an extremely imposing presence: dark-skinned, 6ft 4inches tall, erect, immaculately dressed, retaining that penetrating gaze that others found so discomforting. Walking through the garden centre towards the sanctuary of the cafeteria, he noticed that one of the staff – a cheerful, friendly woman in her late forties, whose knowledge and enthusiasm had previously impressed him – was carefully arranging a display of potted tulips of numerous colours, in varying stages of development, from tight green buds to open, blowsy cups. In the centre, on a raised pedestal, in a sparkling fine crystal vase, was a huge bunch of blood red, cut tulips – the majority fully open, revealing the breath-taking beauty within. In an instant, it was as if his heart ceased to beat, as though he had been dealt a sickening blow beneath the waist, knocking the wind out of him, forcing him to grip the side of the display table to steady himself. Terrifying memories so powerful, so evocative of a time when he was someone else, in a far-off place in a time of nightmare, suddenly overwhelmed him. In a daze, he managed somehow to reach his office, and slump into his chair. A simple display of blood-red tulips was all it had taken to break down the barriers he had so carefully erected and maintained, and thought to be impregnable. Barriers that he had believed would protect him from all that had gone before.

Now he was helpless, his defences breached.

The past poured in.

Unopposed.

CHAPTER TWO

He knew it would not remain so, but that early January morning, following a night when snow had fallen heavily, had begun like any other. He awoke cold and hungry. Normally, he would not know whether he would return to this house or this bed, whether he would eat or remain hungry. Most of the day would usually be spent wandering the empty streets and the parks until darkness fell.

But he knew that this was not to be a normal day.

It came as no surprise, therefore, when his mother told him that he was to go with her. She didn't say where. This was not the first time that he had set off with his mother not knowing his destination, but he had a wonderfully calming feeling that it might be the last.

For as long as he could remember, he had led a life constantly on the move, continually running away from someone or something.

He knew no home.

Often, when there was no money for food or rent, he would be taken – as he was that day – to a relative. But he knew this time would be different. Previously, after a long, silent walk, they would arrive at their destination. A knock on the door, an unfriendly welcome, his mother's well practised speech imploring them to take the boy in 'just for a few days'. The glum reluctant acceptance, the simmering anger and resentment as the days turned into weeks. The quarrels between husband and wife, at first muted, with the wife displaying sympathy to Jackie and the husband hostility, while in hushed and angry tones they would offer their damning verdicts of his parents. He would hear the husband use the word 'throwback' to describe him. In his presence they would discuss the extra cost to them of food for him, and what to do with him during the day. To them, he was 'him'. If they had children of their own, these children would be forbidden to talk to him. It was as if he did not exist. As the weeks passed, the hushed quarrels would turn to heated arguments as the wife hopelessly tried to protect him and the husband's anger boiled over as his authority was challenged. Then the silences; the long, sad silences. Finally would come the ultimatum, and the wife tearfully relenting. The phone call. His mother would reappear, apologetic, nerve-wracked, and he would be taken to the next set of relatives. And the cycle would begin anew.

He accepted all of this with indifference. He harboured no bitterness or rancour towards them, feeling only sadness at their prejudices, their insecurities, and their weaknesses. He pitied them. He knew that these events in themselves were just moments in time, and would pass. Even when he had been sent into dank cellars to scratch amongst the slag for tiny pieces of coal to make a fire, or stand in front of a sour-faced teacher to ask for a free school meal, or sleep with a drunken relative, he always knew the moment would pass and his destiny remain unchallenged. For he knew with a passion that as yet he had not discovered the words to describe, that he was different. He had always known.

He knew that people were disturbed by and suspicious of him. He made them uncomfortable. And he knew why. He looked each morning into the mirror; he caught his reflection in shop windows. It was him, his appearance, his whole being. Even before he had entered his teens, he had stood almost six feet tall, broad-shouldered, and straight-backed. His face was angular, with a pronounced Roman nose, and high cheekbones. His lips were full and sensuous, his teeth perfect. His skin olive dark, and his hair like polished jet. His eyes were coal black, deep set, with long, fine lashes under arched bushy brows. But it was his unyielding gaze that both captivated and repelled in equal measure.

He recalled those rare occasions when a temporary school place had been found for him, and the even rarer occasions when he found himself being admitted to a school for both girls and boys. It was always the boys and the male teachers that recoiled from contact with him, always the female teachers who were drawn to him, and always the older girls who would take him by the hand to a secluded place.

They walked for two hours through ankle-deep snow, without pause and without a word being spoken, before they came to a long line of terraced houses where he vaguely remembered his grandmother lived, as he had been there before. They stood side by side as his mother knocked at the door. He stared at the polished brass lion's head knocker above the number seven.

His first visit must have been in late autumn, because he vividly remembered a long-lived apple tree at the bottom of the garden, with ripened red apples that glowed on the branches. He couldn't have been there for more than a week or so. He recalled being told by his grandmother not to leave the house, to stay in the living room only. He would only see her in the evening when she would feed him and send him to bed at 8pm sharp. When he awoke, the house would be empty. Bread and cheese were left on the table, between two plates.

After a few days, and sensing his boredom, she allowed him to use the back garden – a neglected wilderness of nettles and burdock, with high, uncut privet hedges on either side. In a small shed by the side of the house, he found shears and a trowel. He spent a whole day, until his grandmother re-appeared, cutting back the privet, putting the cuttings into a heap at the side of the apple tree. If his grandmother noticed his efforts, she said nothing. The following day he awoke whilst it was still dark, and came down into the living room where she sat at the table drinking tea. Neither spoke. Immediately after she had left, he began cultivating the ground, digging with the trowel, working methodically on his hands and knees to clear the nettle, the dock, and clumps of grass and long dead plants. Light falling rain made the soil easier to handle. At the end of the second day, unaware of the time and the darkness, he was still working when she arrived home. She looked at his cut and blistered hands, his nails black with the soil, the sweat on his forehead. She called him in and told him to wash. He ate and, worn out by his labours, went to his bed without being told to.

The following day followed the same pattern, and by the time his grandmother returned, the whole of the garden had been turned over. He looked up to see her, dressed in black, standing in the orange glow of the open kitchen door. 'What are you doing?' she asked. He was drawing a furrow in the soil with a stick, and planting the pips from the fallen apples he had eaten. He told her this. She called him in, he washed and ate, and went to bed. The next day his mother arrived, called him in from the garden where he was still working, and they left – only to return much later on this bitter, bleak winter morning.

The door opened slowly, and his mother walked away. His grandmother ushered him in and sat him down at a rectangular pine table. In the middle of the table, on a small, round lace mat, stood a crystal vase full of blood-red tulips. She sat down opposite him, moved the vase to one side, and asked, 'Do you know who I am?'

'Yes,' he said quietly, looking directly into her eyes.

He *had* been in the house before; he *did* know who she was.

She went on, 'Do you know what today is?'

Before he could reply, she said, 'Today you are fifteen. From today, you will live with me, this will be your school, and I will be your teacher. I have chosen you from all of my useless children and from all of *their* useless children,' she explained bitterly. 'I have been watching you, I have had you watched. You are different. You have the blood. My blood and German blood, and from what I'm going to teach you, you will need the German blood more than you will need mine.'

It wasn't until much later in life that he was able to understand fully what she meant when she spoke of the two bloods, hers and the German.

Had she known how quickly the German blood would stain his blood, like ink stains water, and how it could come to rule and control him? And each time he allowed it to infect him, the longer it would take for him to be cleansed? Even in its early diluted form, that which gave him his sense of being different and of supreme wellbeing, even when the life he was actually living suggested otherwise, he was aware of its power. In later years, as he allowed more and more of the black ink to contaminate his system to deal with some real or perceived crisis, or just to sustain him, he realised he was unleashing a rabid dog. Even so, it was with great relief that he was able to call on this Germanising of his blood whenever he felt threatened or in danger, knowing it would make him stronger and more resilient. This new contaminated blood that coursed through his veins, could also – if allowed free rein – make him cruel beyond belief. It gave him a will and a determination that would never abate. Even when in the days to come and the solution was at its strongest, a faraway voice in a faraway place screamed out its resistance, causing in his mind a maelstrom of conflicting thoughts and emotions, a raging unending battle between good and evil.

He hated and ridiculed jingoism, but his eyes would fill with tears at some great patriotic rally or the folk songs of his childhood. He hated uniforms, but would have preened and strutted the moment he pulled one on.

He hated war, but would happily have gone into battle. He knew he could kill a man or men if he thought it right for him to do so, or for a cause he believed in, yet he could not instruct a veterinary surgeon to put down a beloved pet. He hated power and authority yet craved it, knowing he would abuse it more than any man. He hated those who would ill-treat their fellow men, yet could without compunction assist them. Above all, he hated weakness and the weak, yet he also felt a deep, uncontrollable need to be compassionate, to help and comfort those in pain, those who believed their lives held no hope.

Such was the conflict that raged within him, every second, every hour of every day; one that he thought he would never resolve.

Every man was to be his enemy.

And so it began.

For the first three years, he hardly ever left the house. Coal fires were lit on cold days, and no summer days proved too warm for him. Each morning he would begin a regime of strict discipline that never altered. Up at 6am for tea and toast. His grandmother would leave the house at 6.45am in a chauffeur-driven car. Neither would speak. He would then study from 7am until 2pm. That day's books, that day's learning, would have been prepared for him. At 2pm he would eat the four slices of bread and cheese left out for him, then from

2.30pm until 7.30pm, it was further study. His grandmother would return at 7.30pm each evening; never earlier, never later. She would bring food for two – hot in the winter, cold in the summer – and they would eat at the same table in silence; she staring at him, he at the blazing tulips. There were very few occasions when the vase remained empty.

The table would be cleared, and she would fire question after question at him from that day's studying or the previous week, or month or year. She was relentless, yet he proved her choice to be correct. He studied, and he answered with growing confidence, but the more he learned, the more he was expected to learn. Only much later did he realise that whatever he knew, or came to know, his grandmother knew much more.

CHAPTER THREE

It was in the early spring of the second year that his grandmother engaged the services of a middle-aged actress of her acquaintance to give him elocution lessons. 'Because,' she informed him icily, 'the English judge everyone by the way they speak.' Miss Lucy, as he was instructed to address her, had a long, thin, stern face, made up to perfection. Her eyes always seemed to sparkle and dance; her hair, once black, now had streaks of grey. She always wore a full-length black velvet dress, with three rows of white and pink low-hanging pearls, and half a dozen bright bangles on each arm. She arrived and left in a swirl of red cape and expensive perfume.

She referred to Jackie as 'my sweet one'.

She took to him immediately, as he proved to be the perfect student.

He ached to learn. He understood instinctively the importance and power of words and the necessity of expressing them with clarity and beauty. Though no-one had ever engaged him in conversation, he had a mind full of words and a desire to be able to express them. Her task was made simpler because he had no accent that needed erasing.

The days passed easily and quickly. He looked forward to her visits and she to his enthusiasm; she knew he was a starving man set before her banquet. Once she had dutifully completed the formal lesson, she would slowly and deliberately close her book, and break into a wide, warm smile. She would then, to Jackie's delight, begin her telling of stories, of which she was a master, a juggler of words, and images, and imagination. She would tell of the great roles she had played and of the great people she had acted with, her arms a windmill of movement as she stood before him. She spoke of the special theatre where she said beautiful acts were performed in an ugly building, its towering red-brick façade softened only by its reflection in the slow-moving, swan-graced river that flowed by its side. This, her special theatre, lived on the outskirts of a long-ago chartered market town, whose surrounding fields of ripening barley were over-bowed with great green canopies of lime and elm. Each autumn, the horse chestnuts would summon the local children to launch their sticks into the highest branches, causing the nut-brown fruits to cascade over them as they squealed their delight.

The river itself, sedate as an elderly aunt on her way to church, meandered peacefully through the local towns and villages and under stone-arched bridges. At its bank, fishermen would sit statue still, eyes set firmly on the bob-bobbing of the red-topped, line-anchored float. On hot summer days, children would splash at its edge, and lovers lay together in little boats moored and secluded behind a curtain of yellow and green willow branches.

Further upstream, in far-off days, the aristocratic owner of a large country house caused the river to be dammed. This embellished his grounds and gardens, and diminished his reputation. These were, and are, the very same grounds, Miss Lucy reminisced, where as a child she once starred in *A Midsummer Night's Dream*. She and the ensemble were one side of the river, disappearing into and reappearing out of the late evening gloom of the nearby woods. The mesmerised audience was on the opposite side, wrapped warm against the coming chill of the night, sipping from hip flasks, whilst overhead a full moon, low enough to touch, bathed them in a kindly glow. In Miss Lucy's heart, it was always midsummer.

Jackie listened in awe and wonder, his own imagination released from its dark and lonely prison.

On special days, when he had pleased her by reciting from memory a long and difficult piece of prose or poetry, or delighted her by comparing her to a summer's day, she would ask him if he would like to suggest something she could read for him. She knew what he would choose, for she had quickly surmised where his heart lay. Always it would be *Linden Lee* or *The Scholar Gypsy*. She knew what he would choose, because she had made it a habit that at some point every day she would read to him her favourite poems, hoping he would learn to share her passion. And he did.

She read from Browning and Shelley, Lang, Blake, Matthew Arnold, and her favourite sonnets. She recited as if she was on a spotlit stage before a vast adoring audience. Always, eyes closed, she would perform a little bow before transporting herself and Jackie to a lovelier place and time.

Jackie was transfixed, and he never lost his love of reading and poetry, even in those days to come when darkness was never far away.

Occasionally, the heat caused them to take their chairs outdoors. They would sit in the shade of the old apple tree, and Miss Lucy would continue her telling of stories.

It was on these days, no more than six in number, that Miss Lucy would sing *Linden Lee* to him. She had a lovely, light voice, full of emotion and tinged with a certain sadness that Jackie could feel. It was always the same song, and the singing of it deeply affected her. As the final words melted away, tears would fall, unopposed, and she would look upwards from below the apple-hung branches, to the cloudless sky.

It was during the singing of *Linden Lee* that they both heard a loud banging on the front door. She fell quiet and paled. The banging continued, and they could hear someone angrily calling out her name. Together, they went back into the house, and Miss Lucy half opened the door. Jackie could hear the angry demands of a man and Miss Lucy's attempt at quietening him. After a while, she came back into the room looking tired and drawn. Without looking at Jackie, she collected her books and said she had to leave. That same evening over the dinner plates, his grandmother told him, emotionless, 'Miss Lucy won't be returning.' The next morning, as instructed by his grandmother, he returned to his studies.

The following week, the postman handed Jackie a small package. Inside was a recording of *Linden Lee* and a note, which read, 'My sweet one, will you think of me when you play this?' It was signed, 'Miss Lucy'.

Jackie couldn't play it; there was no gramophone in the house. He showed the recording and the letter to his grandmother when she returned from work. She simply said, 'Marx was wrong; it wasn't religion, it was silly, sentimental music. Continue with your studies.'

CHAPTER FOUR

He did as he was instructed. It wasn't until the summer of the third year when, tiring of constant study and feeling the need for fresh air and exercise, with her permission he would leave the house at 5pm with instructions to be home by 7pm, and run the couple of miles to the local arboretum. There he would rest a while, drink from a small water fountain, and observe the exotic birds trapped in their cages. This particular day, though, he was on his guard. He had woken with a very real fear that he was in danger, so released the German blood. He said nothing to his grandmother but prepared himself for any eventuality, sensing danger in everyone he saw and everything he did. He felt no terror, for just as he knew there was danger, he knew he would overcome it.

He was only two or three streets away from home when he turned a corner into a long, narrow alleyway between a row of back-to-back houses, and saw three men halfway down. The tallest stood in the middle of the alleyway, looking towards him; the other two leaned casually against the walls on either side. Beyond them were two women, probably in their thirties, in red and white polka dot headscarves, arms folded.

Without pausing, he carried on walking towards them. When he was less than five feet away, the man in the centre, now noticeably older than the other two, said in a low growl, 'Get him!' and leapt forward. Jackie, turning slightly to his right, thrust out his left arm and smashed his clenched fist into the man's mouth. His head jerked back, and blood spurted into Jackie's face. Jackie felt a sharp pain in his left fist, ignored it, grabbed the man's hair, and swung his head against the brick wall, causing little particles of brick dust to fly free. The other two, falling over themselves to get at him, found the older man, now crumbling and moaning loudly, blocked their way. Jackie let him fall then, stepping over him, made his way towards them. One backed off and the other, seeing him do so, turned back in time to see Jackie's right fist smash sickeningly into his nose. He let out a guttural moan as once again blood spurted. He fell on top of the older man who was now both still and silent, but not unconscious, his eyes wide open, staring up at Jackie. The third man stood off, undecided what to do. Staring directly at him, Jackie took the hair of the older man in his left hand and the hair of the younger man – who was too dazed to prevent it – in his right hand, and smashed each in turn against the brick wall of the alleyway. First the right, then the left, until the third man turned and ran, brushing aside the two women who stood silently watching. In unison, Jackie let the two men fall to the ground, where he stepped over them and, without looking back, approached the women. Neither gave ground.

As he reached them, one said, 'You'd better come with me.' Sensing no danger, he followed her into one of the terraced houses. She led him into the kitchen, filled an enamel bowl with cold water and placed it onto the kitchen table. He watched her without speaking.

She was neither pretty nor plain. She wore little make-up, but had full sensuous lips that were painted red. Standing in front of him, without speaking she reached up and opened each button of his blood-splattered white shirt. Pulling it off his shoulders, she let it fall around his waist. She wrung out a sponge in the cold water and, moving behind him, slowly began washing the back of his neck with long, cool strokes. Coming around to face him, she wiped the blood from his face. Noticing two broken teeth embedded into the knuckles of his left hand, she produced a pair of tweezers from a drawer and removed them. He remained quite still, deciding that for the moment it was all that was required of him. She began to sponge his neck, then more slowly looked up into his eyes, his chest, each stroke beginning just a little lower until finally she reached his waist. At last she spoke. 'You are beautiful.'

Gently, he leaned forward and replied, 'And so are you.' He took her face into his hands and kissed her full on the mouth.

It was almost dusk when he left the house. He hurried home and explained to his grandmother, who was seated at the table with her driver, what had happened. His grandmother immediately dispatched the driver, having first given him instructions. Once he had left, she turned to Jackie and said, 'Were you warned?'

'I was.'

'So you were ready?'

'I was.'

She went over to the sideboard and took out a medicine chest, which clearly had never been opened, and began cleaning and bandaging his left hand. After a while, she said, 'Never be frightened to use your fists to get what you want. But never, never,' she went on, looking directly into his eyes, 'never on a woman. Only men who are frightened of men hit women.'

He was at an age when he believed he didn't have to tell his grandmother everything, so made no mention of the lady. The driver returned, and he and his grandmother spoke at length in whispers at the doorway. The driver, Jackie noticed, did most of the talking.

However, later that evening, just before she retired for the night, half in half out of her bedroom, a tumbler of whisky in her hand, she turned to him and said, 'From now on, find women of a better class. Their morals are just as loose, but their tongues are not.'

The first major change to this routine came about in the same manner as before. One night after dinner, she asked, 'Do you know what day it is?'

'Yes,' he replied. 'It's my nineteenth birthday.'

'Beginning tomorrow,' she said, 'you will have no need of your books during the day, because you will be coming with me. After dinner, you will continue your studies until 11pm. This Saturday, we will begin dressing you like a man.'

Saturday came, and at 6.45am they left the house and walked towards the car.

Normally, he had noticed, the driver would open the door for her, but this morning he was seated behind the wheel. He had learned. Stepping forward quickly, Jackie opened the car door. She stopped, looked up at him, and entered without a word. They drove directly to the best gentlemen's outfitters in the town – a business she owned.

The manager had opened early at her request, and was waiting to greet her at the shop entrance. Suddenly, to his amazement, his grandmother was transformed. Smiling widely, she warmly greeted the manager, shaking his hand, thanked him for his kindness, and apologised for requesting the early opening. Clearly besotted, the manager then shook Jackie's hand – the first person ever to do so. Jackie remembered to make the handshake firm, and the tailor remarked how tall and broad he was.

'And still growing,' his grandmother replied.

The manager's wife arrived with tea in fine china cups. She, too, was greeted enthusiastically, praise being lavished upon her. Jackie tried on various suits, none fitting to the standard required of his grandmother. So it was decided they would have to be made for him. He stood patiently as the manager fussed over him, measurements being taken and scribbled into a little notebook, listening carefully to the conversation between the two women. First, they discussed the business, and once this had proved to be satisfactory to his grandmother, they spoke of families and children. The tailor's wife's face saddened as she spoke of all her difficulties with her and her husband's families. She grew animated and angry as she spoke of the ingratitude of her children, despite, she said, all the sacrifices she and her husband had made for them.

Jackie's grandmother listened sympathetically as the woman poured out her grievances. When she had finished, his grandmother leaned towards her and said, almost in a whisper, 'Fortunate are those whose children merely disappoint them.'

His grandmother chose a pinstripe for the material, deciding it would be three-piece and double-breasted, and that the trousers would have turn-ups. His shirts would be white, his ties blue, shoes black Oxfords, socks black. There would be a white handkerchief in the jacket breast pocket. Little did he know that he would still be dressing this way some 40 years later.

They arrived back at the house at 7pm, having spent the rest of the day visiting farms and factories. They'd stopped off to collect some food, which they then ate in silence. After she had cleared the table and he was about to begin his studies, she quietly told him to leave the studying for a moment and to sit down.

Moving the tulips to one side, she looked into his eyes and for a moment held his gaze, as if hypnotised.

'Tonight we have other things to discuss.' Quickly regaining her composure, she went on, 'Jackie, you are different, and you know you are different.'

'I have always known,' he answered.

'You have the gift,' she said. 'A gift given to few. Some call it prophecy, others destiny or sixth or seventh sense; the name itself is of no consequence. I have it and you have it. You know this?'

'I do.'

'Then you must also know that you must bear this knowledge in silence.'

'I do.'

'You also have the gift of numbers, Jackie, don't you?'

'Yes, Grandmother, but I don't know what my numbers are,' he replied, then added, 'Pythagoras said all of life is numbers.'

She stood up and walked into her bedroom – a room he had never entered – and returned with a jewellery box. 'Stand up,' she said, and as he did so, standing on her tiptoes she placed a gold chain around his neck. It held a Victorian shield-back half sovereign. 'Never take this off. The numbers on the sovereign are your numbers,' she said, and whispered into his ear the four numbers.

'Never forget them, Jackie. Never forget them. If you find yourself threatened or fearful, or if you need a miracle, recite these numbers to yourself over and over again. If someone opposes you, encircle them silently with these numbers. They will never let you down, just as mine have never let me down. You will need their protection, because men will fear and despise you, and women… well, you already know what women want from you.'

She went to the table that stood by the side of her chair and on which stood a tantalus with two glasses; normally there was only one. She had planned for this moment. She poured whisky into both until they were half full, then handed one to him. 'To you, to the future,' she clinked his glass. 'Now I am tired, and I am going to bed.'

At the bedroom door, she turned and said, 'Continue with your studies. Our work is not yet complete.'

The next two years passed almost in a blur. There were numerous visits to the businesses she owned. He had to learn about clothing, and meat, and fruit and vegetables, about groceries, about property, about freeholds and tenancies, and about wholesalers, farms, and land. She owned outright 26 different businesses, each a self-contained limited company, all solid, dependable, and highly profitable. Some she seemed to take a particular delight in. The first visits each morning were to a dozen little cafes she owned. Closed this early in the morning, she would let herself in and empty the contents of the slot machines into a black leather holdall.

'I have a simple arrangement with the proprietor,' she told him. 'They keep all the profits from the café, I keep all the money from the machines. It's a perfect arrangement... for me.'

Her numerous bookmaking shops she also seemed to take a similar delight in. 'The easiest way possible of separating people from their money,' she confided to him.

Once she was confident that he had sufficient mastery of the businesses, she began teaching him about people, warning him beforehand that this was what she excelled at, and if he failed to learn this, he would fail her and himself.

'The first thing to remember is you can be a leader or someone who is led, not both. Most simply do not want to be leaders. Most like to be told what to do; it's easier for them. Why think for yourself when others will think for you? They don't want responsibility. As a leader, people need to believe you are better than them, and they want you to be sufficiently successful to guarantee their jobs but not so successful that you highlight their failures. When you are successful, you can afford to be generous with your time and your praise – the latter is free, and it always works. Smile often; it pleases your friends and disarms your enemies. Accept that everyone who works for you will steal from you – some because they need to, most because they want to. You might, as many do, think if you pay them more, they won't steal. Pay them more and they will steal more.'

She went on, 'When you come to meet charming people, as you will, remember their charm is always in inverted proportion to their honesty. You will meet those who will accept anyone into their circle, provided they have money, and especially if they can make money for them.' On bankers, she had more to say. 'These are the people who sell one-pound notes for one pound and sixpence, and treat their customers with the contempt they believe they deserve for being stupid enough to buy from them.' On journalists: 'Failed authors, who scavenge among the rotting rubbish left behind when the successful and the powerful are shown to be weak and foolish, so that each Sunday, life's failures, reading of the weaknesses of the successful, feel less like failures.'

On the police, she called them 'a tribe apart and under no circumstances to be trusted', adding 'Fortunately most can be bought, cheaply.' She had plenty to say on a multitude of other issues and professions, all with undisguised disgust.

It was during this time, this change to his education, that his grandmother allowed him to listen to the nine o'clock news and be expected to discuss the contents with her, when she allowed herself to vent her fury against politicians.

'When will they realise?' she would groan, after listening to another hopeless mess they were trying to extricate themselves from, either at home or abroad. 'When will these old men learn? When the old men of one country, in their autumn years reflect on the unfulfilled promise of their youth, fail to agree with their like-minded counterparts in other countries, the young men are called forward to die. Better, the old men contend, to die young than to grow old and live as they live.

'And so uniforms are put on, and sweethearts are bade farewell. And they march out to the tune of the bands and the bagpipes. And the young men are sent forward to settle the old men's arguments in a cause they have little knowledge of. And if truth is the first casualty of war – and it is – the weak are the first to perish. The weakest countries are overrun with ease, despite these countries having the bravest and most loyal fighters. The lucky ones will die first, the rest will be sent to places where they wished they had been lucky.'

He had never heard his grandmother speak like this and felt a peculiar sense of pride that she had taken him into her confidence. She rose slowly from her seat, went over to the tantalus and poured out a half full glass of whisky and returned to the table.

With a sigh, she began, 'I fought alongside your grandfather and his brothers, the youngest of whom had been sent ahead to England with our possessions when we realised that we would soon be overrun. Every time I see you, I see your grandfather. We took up arms – simple weapons, guns, rifles, nothing more. We killed many. We should have killed more; we would have killed more, but we were few and they were many.'

Another long silence followed before Jackie quietly asked, 'Then what, Grandmother?'

'We were taken. None of us would ever bear arms again.' With that, as she so often did, she subconsciously tugged at the cuff of her blouse.

Emboldened now, Jackie asked for the first time something that had always fascinated him. 'Why tulips, Grandmother? Why do we always have tulips?'

'Because of home,' she whispered. 'Because of home; my home, your home.'

'And how did it all end?' Jackie asked.

'As it always ends, as it always ends. When the old men are blood sated, and there are too few young men left to die. And when the women call a halt. As someone once replied, when asked why men go to war, "for the women".'

Jackie listened to his grandmother in silence; nothing he in his ignorance could say would comfort her.

Finally, after she had poured herself another whisky, she turned to him and quietly said, 'So now you know a little of my past. And what of you and your future?' And with a knowing smile, she added, 'Poor Alice, how tame her adventures to those in wait for you.'

CHAPTER FIVE

In the following October, shortly after the incident of the fight in the alley, he found himself working at the slaughter house owned by his grandmother – an experience that was to have a profound effect on his life. His very first day gave an indication of what was to follow. Arriving at 6.45am, having made two separate bus journeys, he and a small group of four others were circled around a silver milk churn. The foreman – short, stocky in a white overall, with a fat, round, flushed face, with a square nose etched with red and blue veins – unscrewed the top of the churn. Inside, full to the brim, was pigs' blood. The other boys looked at each other then at him with wan smiles.

'You,' he said, pointing to Jackie, 'taste it.'

The other boys stepped back. Jackie looked down at the foreman, who was a good foot shorter than him, then plunged two fingers into the churn and put them into his mouth. It took every ounce of self-discipline he had not to retch.

'Well?' said the foreman. 'Does it need any salt?'

'Yes,' said Jackie, having not the faintest idea.

The foreman tasted the blood himself, looked at Jackie and said, 'Taste it again.'

Jackie did as he was instructed.

'It needs no salt,' the man said. 'Now remember the taste. This is how it should taste. You will taste each churn every morning.'

They were joined by a tall, thin woman, wearing white overalls, a green waterproof apron, and high, green wellington boots, her hair tied up and covered by a white mesh hat. Incongruously, she wore tiny pink pearl earrings.

'I'm Joan,' she said. 'Follow me.'

She led them to a large water-drenched, stainless-steel table, where another half a dozen girls and women, all similarly dressed, were linking sausages. A tall, oval-shaped machine, with a long, thin nozzle protruding, overhung the table. The top of the machine opened, allowing fresh meat to be poured in.

So began his lesson in how crude and coarse both girls and women could be. To much hilarity, he and the other boys were shown how to put the fine translucent sausage skin over the nozzle. The boys blushed and squirmed with embarrassment as the girls slowly placed the opening of the skins onto the nozzle, then slowly pulled them along until a tight bunch formed at the machine end. The machine was turned on, and the meat poured into the skin and snaked out across the table. Long, loose strands were hung from the front of the boys' waists as the women assessed what they believed to be the correct length. Unsurprisingly, the smaller boys were only allowed a few inches, but for Jackie – to raised laughter and cheers – the length of sausage was slowly allowed to fall to the floor.

On the Saturday morning of the fourth week, Jackie was cleaning the machine when someone switched it on. He felt a sharp pain in his middle finger as a rotary blade sliced into it. Somehow, he managed to extract it, with the end showing a deep red gash. Two or three girls began swearing and shouting at a fourth, who was responsible for the accident, before wrapping his hand in towelling and leading him to a sink where it was washed. Bandages were applied, but the blood was quickly seeping through them.

Alerted by the commotion, the foreman came over, looked at the cut, cursed him, and ordered that he go to the local hospital. Still dressed in his white overall, blood-soaked apron, and wellington boots, Jackie caught two buses to reach the hospital. There, the wound was stitched and re-bandaged.

Two further bus journeys brought him back to the factory where he was met by Joan, who somewhat shamefacedly told him to report to the foreman. Anger contorted the foreman's face as he told Jackie he should not have been messing with the machinery and was lucky not to be fired. Shaking his fist in front of Jackie's face, he told him to go home and that he would lose a day's pay.

That evening, seeing his bandaged finger, his grandmother said nothing. Neither did he. Two weeks later, the foreman sent him into the cutting room. Here, the cheeks, eyes, and brains were removed from the severed heads of pigs, sheep, and cattle. It was filthy, brutalising, and harrowing work – work that tested to the full his resolve and belief in his destiny.

After a while, he was able to carry out the work on the pigs' and sheep's heads. Removing the eyes first made the task a little easier, pushing the point of the knife into the sockets and twisting until he was able to insert his fingers and wrench them out. (He recalled as he did so with little comfort, the vile words of Cornwall.)

The cattle heads, or beasts' heads as they were referred to, were a different matter. Even to him, these were huge, heavy, and awkward to handle. A cut had to be made between the nostrils of the beast, where he had to put his fingers to get a grip. The head would then be hauled onto a large concave block, where the eyes – large, soulful eyes that seemed to silently reproach him – and the long, fat, tacky tongues were the first to be removed. Then came the difficult task of removing the brains. Holding the head of the beast on one side, with the fingers of his left hand in the cut in the nostrils, he had to swing high a heavy cleaver, before crashing it down across the skull forward of where the ears had been. Turning the head to the other side, the action had to be repeated, with bits of blood red skull shaving flying in all directions. The two cuts had to meet in the middle of the top of the head and be sufficiently shattered to reveal the quivering grey brains, which had to be carefully removed before being placed on a tray. The slightest amount of damage to the brains was sufficient to send the foreman into a red-faced rage of fist-waving.

As autumn turned to winter, Jackie's relationship with the foreman and the other men worsened. However, he found a little comfort from the protection of the women workers, whose admiration he had earned with his silence over the incident with the machine. As Christmas approached, a great deal of work was carried out in the bowels of massive deep freezers, in which frozen legs of pork and turkeys were stored. Long days were spent transferring these items into lorries before distribution to the shops. The custom was for chain gangs to stretch from the lorries, out from the bitter cold of the yards into the depths of the freezers, and the items handed from one man to the next. After an hour or so, the men working outside the freezers would change places with those working inside. However, on the foreman's instructions and to the amusement of the other men, Jackie was left for hours on end in the recess of the deep freezers, only being allowed out for lunch – his hair and eyebrows white over, his ears, cheeks, and lips blue from the cold.

He was well aware that his fellow men despised him and the reasons why, and it no longer concerned him. However, something quite unexpected happened that brought into play a new emotion he had not previously experienced.

One late December lunchtime, he, a separate group of men, and a little further away a group of women – arms folded across their chests, smoking and gossiping – were standing outside on the cobbled yard at the factory entrance. A delivery of pigs had arrived for slaughter, and was being offloaded. A small, thin, ugly youth with a high-pitched voice began kicking the pigs as they were driven into the pens. They were squealing, twisting and turning, and crashing into each other to avoid the kicks, their hooves sliding on the cobbled surface, causing their back legs to give way, sending them slipping and sliding on their haunches.

The rest of the men looked on, laughingly encouraging him. The women appeared not to notice. Something in Jackie snapped. Some long, pent-up emotion held in check by rigid self-discipline suddenly erupted. Manufactured indifference to what was happening, his insistence he was merely an observer of events, that he was different, alone and aloof, disintegrated in a second. Blind rage gripped him.

Pushing his way through the group of laughing men encircling the pen, he walked up behind the youth and swiftly, violently kicked him behind his knee, causing him to crumble backwards. Jackie grabbed him by the hair and dragged him away from the pigs. Without pause, he began kicking him – first his legs, then his chest, finally his head. The youth, in a desperate attempt to protect himself, had curled up into a ball. By this point, Jackie was raging, enveloped in a wide-eyed blackness, hunched over the screaming youth, unstoppable.

Jackie picked the youth up bodily, carried him over to the pen, and threw him among the pigs and their urine and excrement. Terrified, the animals scrambled and stumbled in all directions, crashing against the side of the pen, crashing against each other. The youth was stranded in the middle of them, their hooves kicking out at him, their heavy, fat haunches falling on top of him, his squeals almost muffled by the pigs' squeals and grunts.

Jackie turned his back on the pen, and the youth and the pigs, his rage undiminished. At that moment, he was without question quite mad. Through the mist of the madness, he saw the foreman – cheeks flushed, open white overall flapping – rushing towards him. Jackie moved forward to confront him.

On the instant Joan stepped from the throng and stood directly in front of Jackie holding his arms down, pressing all her weight against him. To their horror, everyone could see that Jackie was simply carrying her forward with him. The foreman stopped some two or three yards in front of him. His face was red, his mouth was open, he was panting, but as everyone quickly noticed this was not a look of anger; this was a look of fear. Jackie was edging ever closer to him, unstoppable.

The foreman looked up at the approaching madman, turned on his heels and walked away, quickening his pace as he did so. Joan let go of Jackie's arms and he stood towering over her. She could feel his breath on her face. After what seemed like an eternity, he drew in deep breaths, placed his hands gently onto the woman's shoulders, and said quietly, 'I would have killed him, without a moment's hesitation. I would have killed him.'

'You can't, Jackie,' she said. 'He's been dead for years.'

As the group of men dispersed, each passed him by individually, purposefully looking him in the eye. Each one looked at him differently, each gave an almost imperceptible nod, and it suddenly struck him that although they would always fear him, perhaps, just perhaps, they might in future respect him. He desired neither.

That night after dinner, his grandmother announced that from now until Christmas Eve, he would be working at the turkey farm that she owned. But this time, his grandmother had ordered that he should not witness the slaughter of hundreds of turkeys that had been especially fattened to grace dining room tables on Christmas Day. Instead, he was put in a long, high shed, where new-born chicks were fed and watered. These, he knew, were also destined to be slaughtered. Walking among them as they pecked at his boots, he thought, *Is this what Christmas is all about*? He hated the whole sad, sorry saga.

CHAPTER SIX

It was on his twenty-first birthday that the final chapter of his learning occurred – exactly six years since he had been taken to live with his grandmother. Six years which had seen him grow from a boy to a man; from someone craving knowledge to someone highly knowledgeable. On these special birthdays – for this was the third – he knew instinctively that something unusual would take place.

By now he had adopted a morning routine that had almost developed into a ritual. He would awake early, bathe and dress. He would touch the gold that hung around his neck for exactly nine seconds, no more, no less. He would check that his black Oxford shoes, polished to a glass-like finish, were as clean underneath as on the surface. Fully dressed, he would stand in front of the full-length mirror, checking every detail of his appearance. Finally, he would stand quite still and practise his smile: the full smile and the half smile; the warm, welcoming smile; the cold, intimidating smile. Once satisfied the smile was perfect, he would switch it off. His grandmother would be waiting for him, sitting stiff-backed at the pine table, a cup of tea before her, a cup of tea waiting for him. He would sit down opposite her, and they would both drink. The pleasantries of greeting were not practised. Placing her cup onto the saucer, she would move the full tulip vase to one side as she outlined the day's business.

'Today we are going to the solicitors,' she announced. 'Today all the businesses will be transferred into your name. It won't take long, everything is prepared.' Even by her own standards, she seemed more abrupt than usual, more distant, more preoccupied.

They were driven to the firm's offices in silence: Jackie looking out of one side window; she out of the other. Prior to the actual signing ceremony, almost as if an afterthought, and after the preliminary greetings and handshakes, the solicitor ventured with half a smile, and in a tone that fell just short of being patronising, that he hoped Jackie was fully conversant with the fine details of the documents he was about to sign. Even though Jackie had not seen one single word of the documents, he said with a smile that eclipsed the solicitor's thin-lipped attempt, that he was, adding that he would be returning at a later date to discuss new terms should he decide to continue with this firm. What remained of the solicitor's smile disappeared.

Jackie, and he believed his grandmother, sensed a change of deference. Questions, important and less so, relating to business matters, were now very subtly directed at him, pleasantries and reminiscences at her. As they were leaving, the solicitor took Jackie's hand, almost appeared to offer a little bow, and emphasised that he was always available to speak to and that he hoped he could be of the same service to him as he had been to his grandmother.

It was exactly one month later that Jackie returned home to find the house in darkness. Switching on the light as he entered the living room, he noticed immediately that the vase in the centre of the table – the vase that had, on and off, for six years held exactly 13 blood red tulips – was empty. Propped against its side was a folded piece of notepaper. Opening it, Jackie read: 'So now it's down the rabbit hole for you, to a world beyond satire, a world I have prepared you for. I have taught you everything I know. Continue to learn. You have the gift, use it well. You have the two bloods, mix them well – one to be kind, when kindness is required; one to be cruel. But beware, the more you use the first mixture, the more you will need the second.'

Exercising brevity to the last, the notepaper gave no indication of to whom it was directed or from whom it had been sent. Jackie folded the paper and dropped it into the empty vase, then picked it up, carried it from the living room, through the kitchen and out into the backyard. He lifted the lid of the dustbin and dropped the vase in. Returning to the living room, he walked over to his grandmother's chair by the fireplace, sat down, poured himself a large glass of whisky and smiled. This moment, this feeling, he would long treasure.

He never saw or heard from his grandmother again.

CHAPTER SEVEN

Although exhilarated at his grandmother's departure, he knew he had to resist the urge to make changes to the business. People feared change, so he had decided that for the first few months at least, there would be no change. He also knew that once everyone had concluded that his grandmother would not be returning, the overconfident among them would test him.

He did not have long to wait. His accountant had provided him with evidence that his slaughter house, which supplied his shops only, had begun to supply rival businesses. He had arranged to meet the foreman – the same man who had been in control of the slaughter house when Jackie worked there. It was the first time he had returned to the factory.

Smiling, always smiling, Jackie advised the man of the loss of profitability and asked for an explanation, carefully giving the impression that he was not overly concerned. Sensing weakness, the foreman gave a practised account of falling prices, rising costs, and meat not of the correct acceptable quality being returned or having to be destroyed. Sensing this to be an insufficient explanation, he said he had also recently suspected a couple of men of stealing, but was unable to prove anything. He had, he told Jackie, fired them anyway. He took the risk that he might be asked to name them, but he was not asked.

Jackie had listened to him, nodding his head in sympathy, and said he was sure that the factory would soon return to the expected profit levels. They shook hands, Jackie careful to thank him for the fine job he was doing. He knew instinctively what would happen next. Word quietly spread throughout all of the businesses that he was a fool, who knew nothing, and cared less. He was not, they concluded, his grandmother.

For the next few months or so, as Jackie had predicted, the meat factory's profits returned to normal. Then, in the third month they dropped significantly, as indeed they had at a number of his other businesses. In the meantime, Jackie had instructed his security team to watch both the warehouse and the foreman. Deliveries had begun once again to rival businesses.

The foreman had been regularly visiting the branch of his local bank, and more regularly visiting his mistress in her flat over one of Jackie's shops. He arrived and left the factory in his old car, and transported his mistress to and from expensive restaurants in his new one. Jackie was disappointed, he had hoped his first test might have been a little harder, more subtle, more... testing.

Unannounced, he arrived at the slaughter house early one grey and foggy November morning. Everywhere men hurried between fridges and lorries, their blood-splattered white overalls and aprons in sharp contrast to his own immaculate appearance. The foreman, seeing him, left the cutting room and held out his hand in greeting. Jackie moved towards him, smiling, and held out his right hand, then smashed his left fist straight into the foreman's face. The man screamed and fell to the floor. All activity in the meat factory stopped.

Jackie called over two drivers. 'Pick him up and bring him in here.'

He led them into the cutting room where Jackie placed a chair between two heavy butchers' blocks. He told the men to leave and close the door behind them. They did so without a word and joined the throng of drivers, warehousemen, and girls watching the proceedings through the glass partition dividing the cutting room from the factory. The foreman was slumped in the chair groaning, his head in his hands, blood seeping through his fingers.

Jackie laid his black leather briefcase on the white tiled floor and clicked it open. He took the foreman's right hand from his face and placed it on one block. Reaching down to the briefcase, he took out a hammer and a six-inch nail. He put the nail onto the man's hand and brought the hammer down, nailing the hand to the block. The nail went through his hand very easily, with very little blood showing. As one, the onlookers pulled back from the window as the foreman screamed aloud. Jackie stood over him, smiling.

The foreman clawed at the nail, unable to move it. Jackie went over to the door and invited all the onlookers inside. Jackie walked back to the foreman, who was now looking at him in absolute horror, fearing what was to follow. He instructed the onlookers to form a circle around the foreman, and quietly recited the evidence against him, repeatedly seeking assurance from the foreman that what he contended was true. The foreman, face contorted with pain, nodded his agreement. Jackie turned to the onlookers – men whose job it was to bloodily despatch animals, who now all stood pale and silent.

'Gentlemen,' said Jackie, addressing them with a smile. 'It's much healthier not to steal from me.' He put the hammer back into his briefcase and clicked it shut. He picked out two men and told them to stay, and the others to return to their duties. He gave one of the men a card, on which was the name of a doctor and an address. 'Take him to this address,' he said, 'and leave him there.'

Jackie knew the foreman had too much to lose to complain. The onlookers knew that Jackie knew they, too, were guilty, and would offer no evidence against him. As he was leaving, Joan approached him. She looked tired and drawn, her ugly white, plastic overall and apron hung loosely from her. Her high, green wellington boots made her look ungainly. Her hair was tied up and bunched under a white mesh cap.

Leaning towards him, she whispered, 'Don't end up like him, Jackie.'

'I won't,' he promised. 'I won't.' Moved by her concern, he gently, very gently, brushed the back of his hand against her cheek. Slowly, she tilted her head towards his touch and closed her eyes. He noticed she was still wearing the same little pink pearl earrings. A few days later, Joan received a package. On the bus on her way home, she opened it. Inside there was a string of pink pearls.

No complaints were lodged. Profitability at all of the businesses dramatically improved. His grandmother had instilled in him that the most successful businesses were operated by someone who was adored or someone who was feared.

He had chosen the latter.

CHAPTER EIGHT

It was many years later at a grim little gathering at a late-night Christmas Eve party that they first met. Normally, he would not have attended such a party; in fact, he had only been invited because it was hoped he would not. However, greater forces were at work. For a number of weeks, he had experienced an overpowering feeling that something hugely significant in his life would occur on that day, despite the fact that he hated the hypocrisy of Christmas. He arrived late, a little drunk, and in a sour mood.

It was of no great surprise to him – as it was a frequent occurrence – when a very beautiful, very young woman exited her little circle of friends, crossed the room, and introduced herself to him as Suzanne Lawrence. The act in itself was not unusual, but the way she held his gaze, self-assuredly, was. She was tiny, fragile even, and she exhaled youth and vigour, vitality and freshness, all of which had long since deserted him. Sculptured, ash-blonde hair framed her delicately featured oval face. Bright blue eyes reflected the gaudy green and red baubles that decorated the room. Her cheeks and lips were a light shade of pink. Her mouth gave the merest hint of a sensual pout, which he concluded was too perfect not to have been well practised.

A long, white satin dress hung from her bare shoulders. Her only jewellery was a small, gold crucifix on a filigree chain, which had settled in the nape of her neck, and which, absent-mindedly, she lightly touched when listening, her head cocked slightly to one side. She displayed a level of confidence that only a very expensive education could provide, and spoke in a whisper, causing him to involuntarily bend over towards her and to breathe in the scent of her expensive perfume. Without affecting any false modesty, she told him that she was an artist, a very good artist, that she specialised in portraiture, and she was going to paint his. His only comment on hearing this was to remark sarcastically that she did not have the appearance of someone starving in a garret. Clearly, this observation had been directed at her before, because without pausing she replied, 'No longer a prerequisite.'

'Any relation to that truly great portraitist of the same name – Lawrence, that is, not Suzanne?' he continued.

'No,' she said, smiling up at him, 'nor that little gentleman who liked sand and to be thought enigmatic.'

Finally, smile-less, he asked, 'And are your portraits Cromwellian in nature, or do you flatter your sitters in order to fatten your fee?'

Surprised, and a little disturbed at his mounting aggression and hostility, she moved from one foot to the other, deciding in the little time this afforded her that she would not be browbeaten or apologetic. 'I *am* very fortunate,' she said, 'I can paint who I like, when I like. If I see someone that I find interesting, I ask them to sit for me. Most, I concede, are flattered to be asked.'

Before she could continue, he asked sharply, "And are they still flattered when you present your fee?'

'I don't know,' she replied. 'I never ask. They don't have to sit, or to buy. What I do know,' she continued, 'is that I am probably the best there is at what I do, and you would be surprised at the number of people, both men and women, who resent this. I am too young, too privileged, too clever.'

Then, moving almost imperceptibly closer and holding his gaze, she said, 'Then again, perhaps you resent it, too.'

He opened his mouth to answer but was given no time to do so. She had quickly surmised that he was used to dominating conversations and that only his opinion was of value. She was not prepared to submit to him or his opinions.

'Also, I am a very good businesswoman,' and once again, smiling this time, she went on, 'and you'd be surprised...' She let the sentence die away, before adding, 'I don't suppose you have known many successful businesswomen, have you?'

Unprepared for the answer, she was taken aback when he replied, stony-faced, 'I was taught by one.'

Determined to retain control of the conversation, she went on the offensive. 'As a businesswoman, I am aware that many think all art is nothing more than a commodity, a product to be bought and sold in the marketplace like cabbages, value to be determined by supply and demand, rarity and provenance. I am also aware that there is a very pompous group of self-anointed, self-styled art experts – strangers to their tailors and hairdressers – who speak in a language of their own making. Men and women who believe they are the sole arbiters of taste, and more importantly of price. Their sole purpose is to persuade those people – and there are very many of them who have more money than sense and need to be shown how to spend it. In reality, all these people want to know is one thing and one thing alone: what will it be worth in five-ten-fifteen years' time? To these people, art is simply a form of currency.'

She continued, 'However, as an artist, I believe that any art form can be uplifting and serve as an antidote to ugliness in all its forms. But, like you,' she paused, noticing a softening of his features, his shoulders less stiff. 'Like you, I am a pragmatist, prepared to play the game and, if necessary, circumvent the rules to get what I want.'

'Fame?' said Jackie.

'Money,' she said.

'I admire your candour,' admitted Jackie. He did. To his amazement, he found he was now enjoying her enormously; she amused him, and she aroused his curiosity. Despite her stated pragmatism, he couldn't in all honesty conceive that she was in the least bit a cynic, and this both disturbed him and drew him closer to her. He knew that when a hardened cynic like himself met an innocent such as she, it would always be the cynic that would wither, because the cynic privately wished he could be the innocent, while the innocent never wishes to be the cynic.

A clearer understanding of each other ensued. He was captivated by her intellect and by her honesty, allowing her to talk without interruption.

It was getting late. In a corner, a Christmas tree stood forlornly in a puddle of fallen pine needles. All around them, as she discussed her art and the art of others, tearful little scenes were being played out as lovers discreetly exchanged gifts, hasty last-minute purchases, which would later be secreted away, before hurrying home to their wives and husbands and children. And to the family ritual of Midnight Mass, where they would heartily belt out the carols and pray the prayers.

One group of lovers having departed, another began their goodbyes. The middle-aged men, with thinning hair and fattening waistlines, their cheeks flushed with champagne, would stroke the hair and the cheeks of their young mistresses, whispering once again the promise so often made. Next year, they'd say, would be different; next year, they would be together for good, 'just trust me'. She would then be put into a taxi and sent to the seclusion of the apartment, paid for by him, to spend her Christmas alone.

Jackie watched each heart-breaking little scene in horror. How he despised them and the ugly, sordid tawdriness of it all.

Suzanne noticed he was not listening to her, that he was in a faraway place, an unpleasant place. She lightly touched his arm. 'It's Christmas, why so sad?'

Caught unawares, he winced, and for a moment no smile warmed his face. Then he laughed, hoping she hadn't noticed. She had.

Regaining his posture and his smile, he continued the conversation as if her observation had not been made. He knew, though, that she had witnessed a moment's weakness in him, and it stung. The moment quickly passed and soon they were once again laughing together, the repeatedly replenished flutes of champagne now playing their part to perfection.

As the last of the parting lovers deserted the room, now music-less, deflated balloons and coloured streamers littering the floor, some of the women that had known Jackie looked back over their shoulders at Suzanne and sighed, 'God help her.'

Unaware that they were the only guests left, they talked on until Suzanne noticed the sullen faces of the waiters and suggested it was time to leave. Jackie asked if she would like him to take her home.

Without hesitation, she replied, 'Yes.'

Sittings were arranged but constantly postponed, due to his preference to spend as much of the winter as possible in the Mediterranean farmhouse that he had secretly purchased some years earlier. Consequently, it was in late February that he finally began attending her studio, which, he was not surprised to find, was situated on the top floor in a row of large Georgian mansions. Light poured into the studio from three sides. It was everything he expected an artist's studio to be, with one exception. Leaning against one wall were half a dozen full-size portraits of male and female nudes, their subjects ranging in age from a young man in his twenties to an elderly woman in her seventies.

Noticing that he had spotted them, she said, 'Don't worry, you won't be expected to take your clothes off.'

'How disappointing,' he replied.

He would visit her studio once or twice a week. On each visit, he would take a bottle of champagne; on each visit, he would drink it alone, and in silence, as she worked at her easel. After only an hour or so, she would be forced to put down her brushes, for he was a restless sitter, unused to inactivity. She would remove her apron, wash her hands, and they would settle down together on a large settee, where they would drink and talk. The portrait would always be covered – an unnecessary act, as he showed no desire or curiosity to view it.

Away from the studio, they would visit art galleries and museums. They would go to the theatre and the cinema, all usually at Suzanne's suggestion. Jackie was happy to linger with her over candlelit dinners in his favourite restaurants, where he was known and fawned upon, where they could stay late, and where he allowed Suzanne to talk uninterrupted. He was content to just look at her. He was bewitched by her beauty, her warmth, and her sincerity.

CHAPTER NINE

It was late one sunny morning in early spring, following an evening's sitting that he'd found tedious and irritating, when he decided on a whim to telephone Suzanne and ask her if she would like to see his new country club. He had previously mentioned this latest venture to her, and she had shown some enthusiasm. Readily agreeing, she added that perhaps they could have a picnic.

'Of course,' he replied, 'providing it's in the restaurant of a five-star hotel.'

As the car approached, he saw that she was waiting outside her studio for him. She wore a long, cream summer dress, speckled with blood red poppies, and a wide-brimmed, straw hat. She was holding a small, calf-leather purse in one hand and a parasol in the other. Jackie's mood was lifted by the warming sun, a cloudless sky, and the sight of Suzanne. Entering the car, she leaned towards him and kissed his cheek.

As they left the town behind them and drove into the countryside, the first of the paper-thin spring poppies, their lives as brief as mayflies, lit the grassy banks at the road's edge. A mile or so into their journey, Suzanne suddenly called out to the chauffeur to stop. He did so, and as they climbed out of the car and began to walk back some fifteen to twenty yards, Suzanne reached out and wrapped her hand around Jackie's little finger – a gesture that both moved and delighted him. He had never felt more comfortable in anyone's presence as he did at that moment. They stopped at a rusty, iron farm gate that led into woodland. Spread out before them, under a burgeoning canopy of newly unfurled leaves, was a sea of shimmering bluebells. Lost in the moment, neither spoke.

Once back in the car, Jackie went on to explain to her how, owing to the shrewdness of his grandmother, he already owned most of the land surrounding the grand Edwardian manor house that would be his new casino.

It made good business sense, he said, to bring it – and the land on which it stood – into his ownership.

Before he could go on, Jackie spotted a magpie hopping across an open meadow, causing him to follow the customs of his grandmother, and spit, salute, and call out, 'Good morning, Captain', all of which he carried out with no hint of embarrassment. Suzanne, unaware of such bucolic customs, could only look at him in amazement, while he continued to speak as if the incident had not happened.

The main impediment to take over the manor house in the past, he explained, had been his grandmother's firm reluctance to accept the conditions laid down by the trustees who controlled the sale of the property and land. Lady Laughton, the original owner, had decreed that any prospective purchaser must ensure that the house and gardens be restored to their past glory. However, his grandmother wanted the land to be put under the plough, and the house demolished.

All other potential purchases had been deterred by the possibility that his grandmother could seriously prevent access to and from the house. Stories had been told of broken-down tractors and heaps of manure regularly preventing entry to the property. His grandmother contended, with little conviction, that she had no knowledge of such incidents, and she was therefore content to let the house rot until the trustees accepted her terms. Jackie, though, thought differently.

He knew how easy it was to separate the ordinary man from his money in his betting offices, and he saw no reason why it should be any less easy to separate the rich and the very rich from theirs. He said, only half jokingly, that all he needed was a much grander betting office, and went on to describe the long and tortuous proceedings that had followed. He had proposed renovating the house to the highest standard as a gentlemen's country club and residence, with a fine dining restaurant and a small members-only casino. The grounds would be laid out to Lady Laughton's original plans.

Jackie intended, he whispered to Suzanne, to comply with all of his proposals except one: the casino would not be small. Securing the necessary planning permissions and overcoming the burdensome red tape had been left in the capable hands of his solicitor, Donald Simpson. In order to obtain the licence for the casino, he had again enlisted the assistance of Donald, who formed a new company. He and Jackie recruited a board of directors, consisting of the county's finest, including past local councillors and one ex-Lord Mayor. Two Knights of the Realm and two Lords – individuals rich in land, ancestry, and reputation, but with insufficient income to maintain all three – were also recruited. Each board member was charged by Jackie to recruit the necessary numbers of members he needed.

Each, emphasising the exclusivity of the membership, succeeded. Before the opening night, Jackie had 200 inaugural private members.

The car turned from the main road into a narrow, winding, little-used lane and drove on for a quarter of a mile. Finally it turned left through a pair of intricate, wrought iron gates and along a lime-lined, gravel path to the house.

Suzanne leaned forward over the passenger seat. 'How lovely,' she said.

The house was attractive. Wide and high, it was built of warm red brick that turned blush pink each sunrise and sunset. Attached on either side of the imposing entrance and protruding just a little, each wing was an exact replica of the other. Each of the eight first floor mullioned windows, with sash cords still intact, was beautifully proportioned. On the second floor, eight dormer windows completed the front elevation. Atop the grey slate sloping roof, half a dozen red brick chimneys added to the elegance of the building.

Standing in an elevated position, the house had been built, Jackie told Suzanne, by Sir Ian Laughton – a successful industrialist. The man had quite deliberately sought out and purchased these five acres of farmland and woodland with rich, fertile soil unploughed for decades, in a landscape of mature elm, lime, and oak trees, to please his adored wife who was a passionate gardener. He designed a house to take full advantage of the landscape, agreeing with his wife that no trees were to be felled in the process. His wife designed the garden. The achievements of both surpassed their expectations, and within a decade, both house and garden were considered amongst the finest in the county.

Their two young sons, eight and nine years old before the house was built, shared their mother's passion, and the three of them worked as one to create their little acre of paradise. They called their home 'The Garden House', and any letter addressed as such speedily found its way to them. A south-facing orangery was added, allowing them to grow grapes, peaches, and apricots, and where they could take afternoon tea together. Their father, often away on business, was content with his library and his Labrador.

But nemesis, the enemy of contentment, lay in wait.

War threatened.

War came.

The boys, excited, exhilarated, donned their uniforms.

Their proud parents waved them off at the station.

The first telegram arrived.

Then the second.

Broken of heart but not of spirit, the garden became her refuge. It would be, she determined, a lasting memorial to her beloved sons. Two trees were planted side by side in front of the orangery, their young branches intertwined. She toiled day in, day out. She would sit each afternoon in the orangery at the same little round table they had shared, on which would be three cups and three saucers; in the centre, a tier of cakes and sandwiches. And she would remember.

And when the remembrance became too painful to bear, she would sit beneath the two trees and weep. Some perfect summer days, kneeling, trowel in hand, turning over the dark rich soil, she would look up and see the boys playing cricket on the long lawn, in their white trousers and sweaters. She would hear the hard, red cricket ball crash against the stumps, the cry of 'out' and the protestations and laughter that followed. She didn't believe it possible that anyone could hurt so much.

Her husband, inconsolable, allowed life to leave him. Alone with only her memories and her garden, she refused to be another casualty of the war.

She battled on for another twenty-five years.

The house faded. Neglected, bruised, and ill treated – first, by the convalescing soldiers who she had allowed to be billeted there; later, when the house became a girls' school; and finally, when unloved and unwanted, it was allowed to fall empty and silent.

Eventually, age and age alone defeated her, but not before she had set down the terms for the future of the house and garden.

'To be perfectly honest with you,' Jackie confided to Suzanne, 'it's because of Lady Laughton that I agreed to take all of this on.'

The car pulled up in front of the house. 'Jackie,' Suzanne said, 'please show me the two trees.'

They visited all of the rooms in the house, discussing in detail with the builders and the carpenters the changes that were being carried out. Jackie explained to Suzanne where the restaurant would be sited, where the gaming rooms would be, the private rooms, and finally the upstairs rooms that were being converted for overnight stays. Suzanne listened intently as Jackie, with mounting excitement, walked her around the grounds and showed her Lady Laughton's original plans for the garden.

Wearied by their exertions, they rested under the canopy of a black poplar tree. Late afternoon sunshine filtered through its branches. Jackie stretched himself out on the soft grass and Suzanne lay close by his side, her arm across his waist, her face gently resting on his chest. For a while, neither spoke, content with the moment, comfortable with each other. A pair of red squirrel kittens played in dappled light beneath the wide spreading, low hanging branches of a giant oak. From the grey gloom of the woodland that lay to one side of the house, the intermittent tap-tapping and the mocking laughter of a woodpecker – an echo from the time of Albion – could be heard. Jackie knew his folklore and wondered what this could be a harbinger of. He was soon to find out.

Presently, Suzanne said wistfully, 'I can understand Lady Laughton and her love of her garden. You see, my mother always said that her garden was where she went to be healed. Being away at boarding school for most of the year, I didn't fully understand what she meant, until I was home one summer when I was about eleven or twelve. One night, I was awakened by voices. It seemed as if someone was arguing, far away, very quietly, then I heard "No, Bob, no!", then a loud smack and a crying out. That terrible sound of hand against flesh seemed to freeze me; I couldn't move. Then there followed another smack, just as loud, then another, then another, and all the time a muffled "I can't, I can't".

'The next morning, a Friday, Father had already left for work when I came down for breakfast, which was unusual, as he liked to breakfast with me. He was a director of my grandfather's bank. Looking out through the open French windows onto the garden, I could see Mother, trowel in hand, on her knees bent over a flowerbed, a large Panama hat pulled forward over her face. Before I could call out to her, the maid brought in my breakfast, and in my innocence, I sat down to eat. When I finally strolled out into the garden, I realised quite quickly that Mother didn't wish to face me, turning her head away as I approached.

'Sensing something was wrong, but not knowing what, I bent forward and touched her shoulder. "Mummy, what's the matter?" I asked. Slowly, painfully slowly, she raised her head to look at me. The whole of her face was black and blue with bruising, her eyes so swollen they could hardly open, both her lips cut so badly she could hardly speak, and she was crying. Shocked into action, I rushed back into the house and did the only thing I could think of doing. I telephoned my grandfather.

'After that, everything seemed to happen almost in slow motion. Grandfather and Grandmother arrived first, followed by my mother's two brothers and her sister. My mother was immediately confined to bed under my aunt's loving care, while the rest of the family sat around the dining room table in close intimate conversation. Everywhere there was a sense of disbelief and anger. I heard my two uncles in my parents' bedroom, filling suitcases, deliberating what to pack and what to leave out. Two cases were then deposited at the front door.

'From my bedroom window, I saw my father's car pull up. As he got out, my grandfather's outstretched arms managed to prevent my two uncles from reaching him. Grandfather took him to one side. My father said nothing, but just nodded his head. He was handed the two suitcases. He turned and slowly began walking down the long gravel drive and through the open gate. He didn't look back. I never saw him again.

'Later, when I was sixteen or seventeen, Mother told me that such attacks had been regular. Fortunately I had been at school, and the home helps didn't live in, so she could always escape to her garden "to heal".

'Of course,' Suzanne went on, 'after each attack he begged and pleaded to be forgiven, and he swore that it would never happen again, but of course it did. "He had these needs, you see," said Mother. "These vile needs which he just couldn't control, and which I found beastly." Public schools, she told me ruefully, had a great deal to answer for. "For the sake of our marriage, for what people might think, for you, I tried to carry on as normal. Had it not been for your intervention," she admitted to me, "I'm afraid it might be going on still. You did the right thing, my darling. He was a terrible brute of a man. Do you miss him? I hope not. I certainly don't." Knowing what she wanted to hear, I said, "No, I don't miss him." But I did. I do. To me, he was kind and generous and loving. He took me everywhere – to the zoo, to the cinema, to art galleries. We would have glorious days on the river; Father rowing, me trailing my fingers through the water. Only he knew where the kingfisher dived.'

She fell quiet. Unused to such confidences, unable to offer kind or comforting words, Jackie instead began to talk about his own childhood, something he thought and had hoped he would never do. He spoke first of the hunger and of the cold; always the cold. Even now, he said, he could never shake off the overwhelming feeling of being cold. He spoke of the long days walking the empty, rain-soaked streets, when the grey, low, forever-low clouds never seemed to lift. Of that moment when twilight descended, and the resultant melancholy that overwhelmed him, when the white halo of the street lamps were his only defence against the darkness.

He spoke of seeking shelter and warmth in libraries and museums, where the displaced would congregate, and of the locked and bolted churches with large signs hung from the high-spiked iron railings that protected the church from the outside world, loudly proclaiming 'All Welcome'. He recounted how he would take refuge in bus shelters when the rain became too heavy to ignore. How he would visit parks and arboretums, deserted in the week but rich with the laughter of families at the weekend, and rich in colour and beauty in the summer. And how, on Sunday afternoons, he would sit on park benches listening to the mournful sounds of brass bands.

Finally, how he'd return after darkness to wherever he was staying, and to a bed in a carpet-less, curtain-less, cold bare room. And how in the early, pitch-black hours, with the frost beginning to paint patterns of lace on the windows, he would leave that bed and begin vigorous physical exercises to find warmth. He explained all this quietly without pause and, Suzanne noticed, without bitterness, apportioning blame to no-one. He spoke about the many visits to his relatives and their reaction to him. He talked on and on, lost in that awful world.

After a while, Suzanne reached up and placed her fingers over his lips. 'No more, Jackie,' she said. 'Please, no more.'

Brought back abruptly from his almost trance-like state, he looked down at her and saw she was sobbing.

They had their afternoon picnic as Jackie had said they would, in a grand, chandelier-lit restaurant, with fine linen tablecloths and creamy white napkins rolled in hallmarked silver holders, champagne standing at the side of the table in a bucket of ice. The food was served by courteous and helpful staff while, almost unnoticed, a pianist played Chopin. They ate in silence, each deep in thought. What little conversation there was revolved around the garden.

'Yes,' said Suzanne, 'it would please me enormously if I could help you restore it.' But both knew something had changed between them.

They drove back to Suzanne's home in complete silence, each looking out of the window on their side of the car. That late afternoon the champagne had failed in its duty. They sat apart, only by inches, yet there seemed to be a great, unbridgeable chasm between them that saddened and frightened her. Each had allowed the other a glimpse into their hearts, but only one was beginning to bitterly regret doing so.

She thought for a moment to invite him in, but he was too far away. As she closed the door behind her, she wondered if she would ever see him again. *Had she lost him just at the moment she had lost herself to him?*

He was angry at Suzanne. *Why had she decided to tell him all of that? What good did she think it did? Was it for her benefit or his?* He had no interest in the lives of others. Once again, Suzanne had exposed a weakness in him. Once again, she had caused him to be someone he had no intention of being. This power, this influence she had over him, terrified him.

Arriving home in the twilight, he switched on all the lights and did what he always did when the past intruded on his present; he opened a bottle of vintage champagne. This was a statement to himself of how far he had come. He was no longer hungry; he was no longer cold; he was no longer homeless.

He knew the past only hunted him in the dark and in his dreams. Normally, his fear of sleep meant he trembled for an age on its edge before slowly, too tired to resist, he would lower himself into its emptiness, to sleep just below the surface so that at the first sign of threat he would instantly awaken. But he knew that this would not suffice this night. Tonight, they would lay in wait for him. Tonight, they would drag him down, deeper and deeper, until the light above him turned black. And despite his struggles, the surface would drift further and further away, and he would be lost, and in sleep, forever. His answer was to drink and drink until near oblivion emboldened him then, fearless, he would launch himself into the pit and a darkness so black that even they would be unable to find him.

It was some months before they met again. He had busied himself to forget her. She had busied herself to forget him. Both had failed. He missed her, and she missed him too much. So, on the pretext of having to complete his portrait, they once again began to meet – first at the studio, then at his insistence, in restaurants, or at her insistence, art galleries.

CHAPTER TEN

As the days and weeks passed, he found he was growing ever fonder of her. The way she greeted him on his arrival, her hands resting on his shoulders as she stood on tiptoes to kiss his cheek; the way she softly said 'hello'. When she was painting, he couldn't take his eyes off her, wondering what she was thinking. Her laughter warmed him.

Some nights, when they lay together, something deep and cold inside him began to thaw. Through habit, he always slept on his right side. She would lie on her back, close to him, until hearing his breathing slow and believing him to be asleep, she too would turn on her right side. Then she'd draw herself closer to him, slipping her arm around his waist and whispering, almost inaudibly, 'Goodnight, my darling. God bless you,' before gently kissing the back of his neck. Sleep was no friend to Jackie, and he was amazed how this simple, secret act comforted him. Feeling safe and secure, he allowed sleep to claim him without a struggle. He never told her this.

He liked her in his arms, he liked to kiss her gently on the lips, and they conversed easily like old friends. He looked forward to seeing her, and was sorry when she left. He thought about her when they were separated, having one image of her in his mind – a snapshot mental photograph of the first time they had dined out together; her youth, her beauty, smiling back at him. This was the one image he would never forget, and revisit for the rest of his life. And he was terrified.

She threatened everything he believed in. He had to break the hold she had over him, or her kindness and her goodness would destroy him. He knew what he had to do, but for the first time in his life, he questioned whether it was right.

An opportunity presented itself. After one night of particular tenderness, one of those rare moments when gifts of their secret thoughts and hopes were exchanged, Suzanne half in, half out of a sublime sleep with Jackie's protective arms around her, whispered softly that she loved him. She could not have known the devastating effect this would have on him and on her. He leapt up from where they lay and, towering over her, raged, 'Love is the most debased word in the English language. It's not love people want, it's need, it's lust, it's control, power, manipulation. It's a need to feel, to experience anything that for a second will give meaning to their meaningless lives, that will allow them to feel something, anything. A need to justify to themselves that they are alive and that everything is not pointless, hopeless. They want anything that will quell their fear – a fear that must at all times be buried deep inside them; a fear of everything; a fear of life itself. And they believe – because they need belief, any sort of belief, just to carry on living – that only two things can keep this fear at bay: love and alcohol.

'They begin with love. It's love they are told that they want, that they need, by their mothers, their church, and their God – all of whom demand it back unconditionally, with added interest. They are told they must have children. The truth is they only want children so that some small part of them will survive their miserable existences, some small part of them will never die. These children will pay the price and carry the wounds that are inflicted upon them.

'And one day, seeking freedom, these children will no longer want or need or love them. And when they realise that they are being rejected, that the demanded unconditional love they craved is no longer being returned, they will hit out viciously with an uncontrollable urge to hurt. And the weapon they will use will be guilt, which they will pour over their children like acid. And their children will soon learn that nothing quells that guilt; guilt that becomes a strength-sapping burden that they will be unable to put down. Emotionless, they will play with their children's emotions, pick-picking away at the thin veneer of their conscience until, unable to resist further, their children will submit to their will. And their mothers and fathers will smile the smile of the victorious. They may no longer be loved, but they are still in control.

'Later, these children will become mothers and fathers themselves, and the whole rotten cycle will begin anew. That,' Jackie said, staring blindly at Suzanne, 'is what love is and what love does.'

In the madness of his rage, he ranged from the lucid to the incoherent. The echo of this rage reverberated around the studio, seemingly coming back at them louder than ever. He continued to rant, spewing a new litany of the misuse of the word love, the words tumbling from him, his face grey and contorted with the pain she knew was wracking him.

Eventually, the storm blew itself out, and she watched as he paced backwards and forwards like a trapped and wounded animal.

'And I,' he went on, 'I cannot understand this need to be needed, this great weakness, this terrible childlike weakness. Why do people need to be needed? Why do they need to be loved?'

He looked at her for an answer, but she stared at him blankly, her face drained of life. She was unable to think, unable to understand, unable to answer.

Finally, he was calm. His shoulders drooped forward and he sat down beside her. 'Then,' he said sadly, 'they turn to drink.'

He grabbed the champagne bottle by the neck, reached for his glass and refilled it. Sitting quite still, he stared at the glass, swirling the champagne around and around until the bubbles rose to the surface and, all the breath taken out of them, burst.

'It's where it leads to, you see,' he began, quieter now, weakened by his exertions. 'First the need, the want, and perhaps, for a while, a mutual feeling, a mutual longing is temporarily satisfied. Then one of them realises it is not enough. With good fortune, this will manifest itself early; usually though, for one of them, it does not. And so, in one last despairing act that it is hoped will bind them together forever, the final act of betrayal is committed. And both the rejected and the one rejecting are forced to live with the horror of that one final act, and bear the burden of guilt – a burden that grows heavier by the hour, by the day, by the week, for the rest of their lives. And a child is born from the agony, in agony. Just another child, another unwanted child, an innocent who, born out of the fear of loss, will itself be lost, forever.'

He was spent now and fell silent, head bowed.

A terrible thought brought Suzanne to her senses. She had heard of Jackie's gift and wondered if that was what this was all about. *Was he predicting what would be for them?* The pain of the thought was overpowering. She wiped the tears from her eyes. *God help me*, she pleaded silently. Then, seeing Jackie and his pain, *God help him. What terrible midwinter storm is raging inside his head? He cannot know how much I love him, or he does, and the thought terrifies him? I will never hurt him. I will never betray him. My darling, my poor, poor darling*, she thought. *What have they done to you? What have they done to you?*

She never again mentioned the word love.

From that night onwards, he cynically and systematically began the dismantling of her confidence, her ability, her belief in herself, in her art, in him. Each sitting became a battleground, a battle to free himself of her hold over him – he seeking any excuse to wound her; she refusing to be wounded.

He needed her to hate him. He deliberately began to miss appointments, or he would turn up late and abuse her, picking fight after fight. He told her to finish the portrait quickly so he could burn it. He criticised her dress, her make-up, her art, her privilege. He would send her a bouquet of flowers and a note that simply said 'Sorry', only to begin the process anew. Her response to all this only deepened his resolve, for she remained dignified and friendly, greeting him with the same gentle kiss and never meeting his bile with bile.

After a few months, he realised that he was losing. She was pitying him, understanding of him, forgiving of him. So he stepped up the assault. He arrived late one night, drunk, hammering against the door until she opened it. At last he saw fear in her eyes. He ranted at her, throwing open paint pots against her canvasses, smashing the easels to the floor.

At last she could take no more. Sobbing uncontrollably, she beat her hands against his chest.

'What have I done?' she said. 'What ever have I done to you? All I ever wanted was to love you. You hate me for loving you.'

He looked down at her in horror, ashamed and sickened at his brutality. But he had won. *Now she will hate me*, he thought. *Now I will be free of her.*

Outside the studio door, he stood for a moment, conflicting thoughts causing his head to spin. He rested his forehead against the cool, marble wall. He could still hear her sobbing, then 'God bless you, my darling. I love you.'

He suddenly felt a pain he had never felt before, as if a knife had been plunged into him. Then he found himself strength-less, crumbling into a heap on the floor, sobbing for the first time in his life.

His chauffeur-driven car was waiting for him. He turned his collar to the wind and rain and climbed into the back seat. On the journey home, the car was forced to stop at traffic lights. Glancing down at the rain-swept pavement, glowing in the red light, he saw that a sparrow had fallen. It lay quite motionless. At its side, another sparrow was frantically hopping around it, gently prodding it with its beak, as if pleading with it to get up. It continued doing so hopelessly for what seemed like an eternity, until the lights changed and the car moved on.

He heard nothing from Suzanne for nearly a month, and hoped that would be the end of the matter.

It was not.

He received a note from her, advising him, in almost business-like terms, that she had completed the portrait of him, and he would be welcome to view it any evening. He had no interest in the portrait and would not purchase it, though in truth he realised Suzanne would never give it up to be burned. He thought of sending a note back asking her to send the completed portrait to him with her fee, but that would be cowardly, and he knew that he wanted to see her again. He arrived late one evening, having drunk a bottle of champagne, carrying another for them to share. He was determined to be congenial. He would admire the portrait and remind her, kindly of course, that she had promised to make a gift of it to him.

But that was before.

She greeted him warmly, her hands on his shoulders, a kiss on his cheek, a smile… but a chilled smile, and she did not look into his eyes.

She led him over to the covered easel, and when she was convinced he was standing exactly where she wished him to be, she removed the cover and watched his face. For a split second, shock froze and sobered him. The whole of the canvas, with the exception of the eyes, had been painted over with thick layers of white paint. The eyes seemed to leap out from the canvas – hypnotic, black, cruel, dead, daring the viewer to look into them, drawing them in, drowning them.

He found himself looking into his own eyes, into his soul, into that deep, frozen part of him that he refused to believe existed. And he was repulsed by what he saw, by what she saw.

'Now,' she said coldly, 'you may leave.'

CHAPTER ELEVEN

The affair, if that was what it was, was over.

He retreated to concentrate on doing what he did best. All his thoughts, all his energy, to be concentrated on the opening of his country club and casino.

But it was not the end of the affair.

Carefully orchestrated rumours of a new art form were being circulated. Suzanne and her uncle, the gallery owner – a man whose only talent was money-making – and a few of his closest confidantes, who shared the same talent, had devised a plan and it was now time to put that plan into action.

Suzanne's army of pompous, self-anointed arbiters of taste and price were being mobilised. In college halls and private quarters, dons proclaiming themselves to be in the vanguard of a new art movement, held court, dispensing tea and cake to small groups of impressionable undergraduates. High-born hostesses in Mayfair mansions gave dinner parties for the self-proclaimed intelligentsia – those who normally only met to reassure each other of their superiority, and could be relied upon to do their hostesses bidding.

In expensively located galleries, where beautiful long-legged ladies posed among oversized paint-splashed canvasses, the gallery owners – elegant middle-aged men with gardenias in their lapels – sniffed the air and picked up the scent of money. A quietness of auction houses, those modern temples to man's greed, where no shame was attached to proffering inducements to nervous clients, lent their covert support. In select little gatherings held in cramped rooms above musty bookshops, those who printed expensive, rarely read, seldom bought magazines, inked their blocks and made ready their presses.

Others met at those gatherings of the languid and the bored, where any new topic was manna to those to whom time was a commodity in endless supply, and madness a mere moment away. All now had something to unite them, something to discuss, and 'art' was a topic worthy of their attention, their intellect, their status. All were anxious to play their part. After all, hadn't they been told that not only was Suzanne, who was by now being described in almost mystical and reverential terms, talented and beautiful, but also that she was 'one of them'? A head of steam built up. Suzanne's army may well have been strangers to their tailors and hairdressers, but they were no strangers to the proprietors of the leading newspapers and magazines of the day, nor to the makers of radio programmes. These were the ones who believed they owed it to the people to force-feed them with what was good for them. And what was good for them was 'Art'. These were the ones who believed it to be their moral duty to enhance the empty lives of their readers and listeners with 'culture'.

Lengthy articles to generate public enthusiasm were written by excitable art correspondents of local and regional newspapers. Radio programmes were broadcast, in which learned art historians and critics, famed among themselves, pulled at their pipes and aired their views in solemn tones. All agreed that a totally new art form usually appeared every thirty or forty years or so, and the time was now opportune for a new artist to burst onto the scene. They went on to confirm that they had viewed the work of an exciting young artist, whose talent displayed a level of maturity and imagination that they had never before witnessed in one so young. Some were struck, they said, by the stark beauty of her work, some by her bold brushstrokes, but all by her unique interpretation of minimalism. All agreed that her exhibition would be the highlight of the year.

The fact that none of them had as yet seen Suzanne's new art form was deemed irrelevant. Whatever they described as great art *was* great art.

Newspaper advertisements were produced to arouse the curiosity of the indifferent, and once it had been decided that sufficient interest had been generated, it was announced that there would be an 'Exhibition'.

A date was announced. The place, a fashionable Mayfair gallery. The name of the artist, Suzanne Lawrence. Suzanne knew her talent remained unchallenged, but as she had stated, she was a businesswoman and she wanted to be rich, so she too would play her part.

Two weeks prior to the opening day of the exhibition, the large bay window of the gallery where the exhibition would be held, was totally blacked out from top to bottom, from side to side. Passers-by stopped to look at the window, pointing and discussing what might appear. Cars and buses slowed to a crawl so that passengers could do likewise. On the day of the opening, following an extensive advertising campaign, a huge crowd had gathered. People spilled over from the pavement onto the road, bringing traffic to a standstill. Those on the top deck of immobile buses rushed to the side closest to the gallery window.

At exactly ten o'clock, the gallery owner – Suzanne's uncle – directed a team of beautiful young girls, all dressed in long, white, silk gowns, with white shoes and white turbans, to begin slowly and deliberately to peel back the black coverings from the inside of the bay window to reveal a great white space from top to bottom, side to side, save for a thin, black-edged border.

The gallery owner – a master of the theatrical – had dressed the whole inside of the bay window with white silk. Almost invisible in the centre was a white painted easel; on the easel, a white frame also covered entirely with white silk. Outside, the crowd gasped, some applauded. Those amongst them who considered themselves more knowledgeable than the rest, remarked learnedly that this was the modern antidote to Malevich's iconic stark and revolutionary work that once changed the way art was perceived. This was, they said, to be the new way we looked at art. Those less knowledgeable around them nodded sagely.

'A new icon for the new era,' someone from the crowd shouted, and again they began to applaud. Before the applause had died down, Suzanne appeared through the silk backcloth. She was also dressed in a long white gown, though no turban for her, and she stood at the side of the easel with a smile both innocent and knowing. Pre-warned, the photographers from all the national newspapers primed their cameras. The crowd, the majority of whom could see nothing, fell into respectful silence.

With a nod to the photographers, Suzanne removed the white cover to reveal her portrait of Jackie. A moment of astonished silence followed, broken only by the sounds of the clicking cameras. Those who had earlier espoused their Malevich theory, fell quiet and slunk away. There followed a communal gasp, then wild, unending applause led by those in the crowd placed there by her uncle to do so. Those who were instructed to shout out, 'Magnificent. Marvellous. Unbelievable' did so. Those who wore hats threw them in the air. Those at the back cried out, 'Let us through, let us through.' It was left to the police, who had been informed the previous evening that there might be some disorder, to pacify the crowd and see them on their way.

That evening, and the following day, a Sunday – the best day for the reading of appreciable articles, her uncle had said – the reviews appeared, all pre-written and presented to the editors in good time for publication. The self-anointed had excelled themselves. Thesauruses had been raided; dictionaries devoured. Earlier, lots had been drawn among them, and a certain number of adjectives and quotations had been allocated to each of them to prevent duplication. They agreed that the inclusion of a Latin phrase or a French quotation would be permitted, provided neither were translated. This was, they all agreed, to be the new art movement, henceforth to be called 'Art of the Soul'. Art free of all incumbents.

True art.

Exposing our souls for all to see.

Our innermost thoughts, our true lives.

Us as we really are, exposed.

Art of the Soul.

The downmarket newspapers quickly decided to settle on 'Eye Paintings'.

Jackie read the reviews and was horrified at Suzanne's betrayal of him, even though she had not named him as the sitter. Her actions proved to him that for once he had been used more than he used. His admiration of her grew.

From that opening day on, Suzanne's uncle placed two guards on the outside of the gallery – one either side of the window. All day and all night, the gallery window remained lit. Newspaper editors used their influence to gain exclusive interviews with Suzanne. All, as had been previously arranged, had their wishes granted. All headed their interviews 'Exclusive'.

What everyone wanted to know was, who was the sitter? Suzanne didn't need her uncle to tell her that keeping the identity secret would make the painting far more mysterious than exposing the sitter. So she declined all offers to tell. There were those, though, who thought they did know, and were only too happy to tell – for a price. And so the story grew and grew; editors, desperate for a scoop, resorted to all means to obtain the sitter's identity. Money changed hands. Fearful of the libel laws, however, the editors left it to the gossip columnists and their less than subtle hints, quoting the friend of a friend, or so and so alleges, or, more commonly, making a point of recording all of the evening activities of Jackie alongside those articles about Suzanne.

However, Jackie was never identified as the sitter. If no editor dare publish his name for fear of libel, no source dared to be named, for fear of Jackie.

Crowds continued to gather at the gallery. Tourist buses changed their routes so that all nationalities could tell their friends at home that they had seen the 'Eye Painting'.

Suzanne's uncle played his next card. He called a press conference at the gallery, with Suzanne in attendance, to announce that an anonymous buyer had offered a seven-figure sum to purchase the 'Eye Painting'. He paused for effect, and for the cameras to click, then looked at Suzanne. Appearing both perplexed and a little uncomfortable – actions well practised beforehand – she said she wished to make it clear that the painting was not for sale and would never be sold, for any amount of money. Both Suzanne and her uncle knew no such offer had been made, but nevertheless the story made headline news.

Now the guessing game was who had offered a million pounds for the painting. The rich and famous were sought out. None wished it to be known they disliked art or didn't have a million pounds to spare, and their 'no comments' fuelled the fire. Finally, came the master stroke. Another press conference, this time broadcast live, the radio stations having been informed beforehand that a very important announcement would be made. At this conference, her uncle, in a cold, business-like manner, announced that a bid in excess of three million pounds had been offered and rejected for the original painting, but because of the incredible interest shown and to further this new 'art form', Suzanne had agreed that she would consider commissions for six other portraits only. Anyone could apply, but Suzanne alone would make the final decision.

In total, therefore, her uncle added, taking over the microphone, there would only be seven masterpieces of this new art form by Suzanne Lawrence. Each successful applicant must guarantee that no copies or prints be taken of his or her portrait. Each portrait would be signed and numbered to seven and the work completed within two years. There would be no further portraits painted by Suzanne on this subject, ever.

This carefully crafted commitment was made to emphasise the rarity, and thereby maximise the price of the paintings, and did so.

It was also a carefully crafted lie.

Suzanne and her uncle had already agreed that once the six new commissions had been completed, she would commence work on a new series of seven eye paintings that would be entitled 'The Unknown Sitter'. Then, after a great deal of excitable enthusiasm had been generated by her uncle and his associates, they would be distributed through selective galleries and auction houses, as would the resultant signed and numbered limited-edition prints. Once this had been proven to be highly successful, which it would be, Suzanne would quietly retreat into semi-retirement, to be brought to her easel only at the behest of some very rich individual, who would happily sign a confidentiality agreement in return for being the subject of an 'Eye Painting'.

Less often, to accommodate the wishes of some highly paid chief official of a registered charity, she would agree to produce a small number of 'Eye Paintings' themed around the aims of the charity – usually the pleading, pain-filled eyes of some emaciated black child in an impoverished African country. The painting would be auctioned and the proceeds, some of the proceeds, would benefit the charity concerned, if not the children. The highly paid, chauffeur-driven, pension-cushioned chief executive officer, slyly suggesting an honour in the offing, emphasising to Suzanne his charity was too poor to offer any payment.

But that was for the future. For now, as expected, the world's richest men and women competed for the honour of being painted by Suzanne, and for the chance of being the owner of a very unique and limited edition of a work of art. A work of art of themselves. Mysterious gentlemen arranged appointments, Suzanne insisting they meet at the gallery so that their expensive limousines with blacked-out windows would be seen parked outside. Her uncle allowed himself to be photographed secretly entering and leaving foreign embassies, his hat pulled down over his eyes. Representatives of church leaders from a dozen different denominations congregated to extol the saintly virtues of their respective leaders. They could offer no money, they said, but believed Suzanne's generosity of spirit would ensure that she would choose their chosen one. All said they would pray that she would make a decision in their favour. Their prayers went unanswered. Dictators of drought-ravaged countries dispatched their finance ministers by private jet to expensive hotels where Suzanne's uncle was asked how high from the top of the coffee table a stack of five-pound notes would need to be for their application to be favourably received.

The beautiful, brittle young wives of very rich, middle-aged businessmen insisted they apply and, unused to failure, set about organising celebratory parties. Those who had a great deal of money to offer, but nothing else, offered a great deal of money.

Suzanne and her uncle had already decided that the winners would all be of unimpeachable character and would own or control the world's biggest banks, businesses, or institutions. They would be elderly and immensely rich. However, they had also decided that applicants who had none of these attributes, and may have amassed their fortunes by unconventional methods, would still be considered if their bids far exceeded all others.

And they had evaded capture!

Less than a month before they were to reach their decision, however, an event occurred that would alter the outcome.

Lady Dorothea – Dotty to her diminishing circle of friends – was an extremely rich woman of a certain vintage, and the only child of a disgraced beer baron. A man unwise in pursuit of his pleasures, he had chosen antipodean exile in preference to a tumbler of whisky and a silver-handled pistol, leaving her fatherless and alone. Some years previous, her mother had bolted with a jump jockey – a sandy-haired, freckle-faced Scotsman who had been prevented from competing in a kilt on the grounds that he, a Cameron, should not wear the tartan of a Macdonald.

Unrepentant, he sought redress by riding out each Sunday on Rotten Row, sporting the Macdonald tartan. In deference to the Sabbath, he rode side-saddle. Lady Dorothea's mother, however, deferred to no-one. She rode by his side on her highly polished Arabian black stallion. Behind them were two huge, grey, mad-eyed Irish wolfhounds on leather leashes, steaming from their exertions, panting, their long pink tongues hanging limply from the side of their salivating mouths. Ahead, a lone piper in full Highland dress, sporran swinging, blew out a mournful lament.

Sometime later, the Scotsman and his mistress left for the Cape, to grow oranges.

Lady Dorothea became famous for collecting diamonds and husbands, particularly those of her friends. She lived, spoke, and dressed as if it were 1922 – the year she came out as a deb, and her whole world sparkled. A great partygoer and giver, she held boredom at bay with a succession of adventures that were both illegal and immoral. Decades passed, of which she had no knowledge. The banning of mirrors from her various households and her short-sightedness spared her from seeing the effects on her face and body of her lifelong activities and addictions. In middle age she had subsisted on young men and alcohol. Eventually, when neither could any longer stimulate her, she gave up on both and felt the better for it.

Experiencing modern life for the first time, she quickly decided 1922 was preferable, and so remained there. She came to philanthropy late in life, at the insistence of her accountant, but came to embrace it and the enthusiasm of the young artists she was able to help. They in turn gave her something she had never had – true friendship. They adored her eccentricity, protecting her and it. It was they who, aware of Suzanne's proposed painting, persuaded Lady Dorothea that she must become a candidate. Unwilling to disappoint them, she sent her butler, the only man she had ever trusted, to meet Suzanne.

The vintage Rolls Royce drew up outside her gallery and the butler stepped out of one world and into another. Unaware of how to address a butler she had never met, in a situation she had never envisaged, she led him into a small, back office, and although unsure of the correct protocol, decided to offer him tea. A china pot and two cups were discovered and presented on a silver tray. He insisted on pouring. Tall, with a pronounced stoop, it quickly became apparent that he occupied the same time period as his mistress. He alluded to Lady Dorothea's many important and powerful friends, Lady this and Lord that, the Duke and Duchess of wherever, and of course, he became conspiratorial, 'Milady is a personal friend and confident of Mr. Balfour, the Prime Minister.'

To her surprise, Suzanne accepted all of this as fact. He went on to list all of the causes she had supported and all of the artists she had helped. She was, said the butler, a good, kind woman, and he sincerely hoped Suzanne would accept his nomination of her so that she at last would be recognised. Suzanne listened quietly without comment, without interruption, hypnotised by the butler's impeccable manner, perfect diction, and absolute sincerity. He thanked her most cordially for receiving him and handed over an envelope sealed with red wax stamped with *fleur-de-lis*.

As he was leaving, he turned slowly to face Suzanne. 'If I may say so,' he began, 'you remind me so much of Milady, so beautiful, so very, very beautiful.'

Suzanne was not offended by his remark. She realised that he, like everyone, wished to only remember the faces of those they loved when they were at their most beautiful. She decided there and then that she would paint Lady Dorothea.

At the height of the frenzy, the final press and broadcast meeting was convened. This time, the world's press had gathered. Sealed bids had been called for and over six hundred received. The gallery and the road outside were besieged. With purposely understated ceremony, Suzanne – after an opening address by her uncle – slowly and deliberately read out the name of each successful candidate. Each name was met with a gasp and a round of applause.

Those who had failed in their attempt quickly let it be known they hadn't applied, after first being given an assurance by Suzanne that she would neither deny nor confirm such statements. Not everyone rejoiced as the winners were announced. Brittle young wives were broken, their parties hastily cancelled, favours for their failed husbands withdrawn. The minions of dictators sought asylum, fearful for their lives. Suitcases full of five-pound notes assisted their passage to freedom. Those whose prayers had not been answered found solace in the arms of atheists.

During this time, other artists were being directed by their agents and patrons to embrace this new art form. All let it be known that they, too, were prepared to accept commissions for an 'Eye Painting'. This proved to be a resounding success. Galleries were suddenly filled with 'Eye Paintings', all with the artist's individual interpretation. One enterprising young lady, sensing an opportunity, caused a mild sensation by painting a pair of porcelain-like hands, shot through with raised blue veins, that seemed to be reaching out towards a white canvas, holding at bay something both unreal and deeply disturbing. Between the open elongated fingers, with their sharpened blood-red nails, it was just possible to make out Suzanne's painting of Jackie.

Religion proved a most lucrative market. Eyes of the Disciples, Popes, and holy men in particular, proved most popular, each painting highlighting the character, good or evil, of the individual. Even more popular was the work of a wildlife artist, who produced paintings of the baleful eyes of puppies and kittens and baby seals to mass adoration. Posters were produced in their thousands to decorate the bedroom walls of adolescent schoolgirls. Subject matters ranged from month-old babies to old men with rheumy eyes. All works in this new genre were entitled 'Eyes of…'.

Finally, a sub culture sprang up designed to mock the new cult, the new religion, of the 'Eye Paintings'. This new breed of anti-artists turned their attentions and their limited talents to other parts of the anatomy, and in doing so left no part of the anatomy unmolested.

Middle-aged artists who had learned the art of money-making concentrated on producing these less often seen parts. These also proved immensely popular. Priced sufficiently high to prevent them from being classified as distasteful, they quickly found their way into the private collections of the too rich and the aristocracy.

Within two years, all but one of the 'Eye Paintings', as they had come to be known, would be hung in the panelled boardrooms of the world's most successful companies.

As for the original Jackie 'Eye Painting', he was told many years later that it had been purchased from Suzanne by a very senior member of Her Majesty's

Government and discreetly presented to the black dictator of a small African country, where oil had recently been discovered. It was hung in the dictator's office from a huge mahogany panelled wall, underneath which was an elaborately carved ivory table where the dictator proudly displayed a collection of the shrunken heads of his enemies. A few days after the presentation, it was announced that a contract had been signed giving Britain the sole rights to the country's oil.

Back in Suzanne's studio, in a darkened corner, stood a white easel. On the easel was a portrait; the portrait was covered by a white cloth.

But it was still not the end of the affair.

It was Jackie's instinct, an instinct that had never let him down, that had dictated he should attend that Christmas Eve party where he had first met Suzanne. He could not, and would not, accept that his instinct had failed him. He wasn't concerned about the portrait; he had treated her appallingly and probably deserved what had happened. In fact, he approved of the way she used the situation to her advantage and the way she had fooled everyone, including him. And the manner in which she had made a fortune for herself, only increased his admiration of her. Nothing could persuade him that later – not now – they would be together again. She had awoken something in him that he was unable to name nor understand. Neither could he understand how no day could pass without him thinking of her. He believed, and it was a deeply held belief, that Suzanne was the only person he had ever met who would never hurt him.

What happened next, therefore, shook him to the core, causing him for the first time to question what he had never before questioned. A letter was delivered to his office marked Private & Confidential. He opened it and a small black and white photograph fell onto his desk. It was a photograph of Suzanne cradling a newborn baby, shawl-wrapped in her arms. Suzanne looked radiant, beautiful; achingly beautiful. The baby, pure, innocent, perfect, silently slept.

On the back was written:

Our baby
She is called Catherine
I love you Jackie
God Bless You.

Jackie reeled. He stared at the message, stunned. The room swam before him and he thought he was going to faint. The photo slipped from his grasp and fell to the floor. Slowly, very slowly, he regained his senses. Then he raged. He wanted to smash, to destroy everything in his sight. Everything within his reach he picked up and threw against the wall, upturning the furniture, kicking over vases, every glass and bottle in his cabinet he smashed to the floor.

Never again would he trust anyone. Never again would he allow himself to be close to any woman. Nothing had changed. Men hated him; women used him. That was how it had always been, that was how it was, that was how it would always be. He was, he now admitted, wrong about her; his instinct about her had been wrong. Worse, much worse, he now realised, too late, how much she could hurt him.

Calmer now, he walked to the office door and opened it. His secretary looked up. 'Have that lot cleaned up,' was all he said.

CHAPTER TWELVE

All the time Suzanne had been engaged in what Jackie dismissively called 'her little adventure', he had been totally absorbed in the opening of his new country club and casino. Once again, Jackie instinctively knew that this would be perhaps the most important event in what had already proven to be a most eventful life. He also knew that great danger attached itself to this enterprise, though he was given no insight from where or from whom this danger would come. As a consequence, he allowed his blood to be diseased. He knew he would never be able to relax with either the club or anyone or anything connected to it. The only certainty was that at some future point, as yet undisclosed to him, it would lead to a major, if not *the* major change to his life.

Nevertheless, he knew he had no choice but to go ahead. The club opened without fanfare or ceremony, Jackie believing that privacy and discretion must be rigidly observed at all times if success was to be achieved. Each of the specially selected two hundred inaugural members who had paid handsomely for the privilege, and would be expected to continue doing so, received a personal invitation. There were seven official opening nights, with each member allocated a particular night. None failed to attend. On arrival, each was greeted by a board member and offered a glass of vintage champagne, each glass engraved with the name of the club, 'Laughtons' – nowhere else was the name to be seen – prior to being escorted to the restaurant and served a five-course meal. Dinner completed, each member was given gaming chips to the value of twenty-five pounds and shown into the casino. Certain 'Elite' members, as they would come to be known – each personally selected by Jackie – would also be allowed to spend the night in one of the twelve luxury rooms which had been converted, each with its own private entrance. On the ground floor were rooms where intimate parties could be held; these, too, could only be arranged through Jackie.

The majority of the personnel, especially the croupiers, waitresses, and hostesses, were young women. All wore long, black sleeveless dresses, cut high on the thigh and low at the neck, around which hung a single row of pink pearls. All were beautiful. The few men employed, mainly for security purposes, could best be described as handsome, though some among them could match the women for beauty. Jackie was aware that not all of his guests shared the same tastes.

It quickly became apparent that Jackie ruled 'Laughtons' with iron discipline and absolute discretion. As confidence in it and him grew, so did attendance, and so did revenue. Jackie's only interest in the restaurant and its unparalleled selection of fine wines was to ensure that it mellowed the members into his casino. This was where the real money was to be made.

Jackie preferred to operate from the shadows, and the only occasion when he was visible was when someone won a substantial sum of money and wanted everyone to know about it. Relaxing after his win in a private room set aside for such purposes, on a large leather Chesterfield, with a smiling hostess either side of him, surrounded by his friends, well-wishers, and the envious, the lucky member would wait patiently for the arrival of Jackie, who would enter the room with a flourish, brandishing a cheque and a wide smile. Two hostesses would accompany him, one carrying a jeroboam of vintage champagne, the other a tray of 'Laughtons'. To much cheering and loud applause, the hostess would pop the cork and pour the wine. Jackie would shake the winner's hand, loudly reading out the amount of the cheque, then quietly leave the room to the revellers, content that the money was only being loaned.

Despite it being well known what type of person Jackie was, and the way he ran 'Laughtons', there were still those who thought his standards did not apply to them. One evening, after the club had been opened for about three months, a young man who Jackie later discovered was the third and dissolute son of an Earl, and who had recently been allowed to return to the country after a period of enforced parental exile, had been brought to the club by a member who was later to regret doing so. The young man was disadvantaged by a shortage of stature, eyes that testified to a glandular malfunction, and an about-to-burst boil that strived to free itself from the constraints of a tightly fitting, stiff, white wing collar. Having lost not an inconsiderable sum at roulette, he turned away from the table in a tantrum, his friend unable to calm him as he shouted that the wheel was fixed and that the croupiers were crooks. He suddenly noticed Jackie who was stood quietly in the background.

'My God,' he exclaimed far too loudly, in a voice that despite his age had contrived not to break, 'I thought this was an exclusive club.'

All around, silence fell. Drinks were halted on their journey to lips. Conversations ceased mid-sentence; wheels were prevented from spinning. Members and guests alike looked first at the young man and then at Jackie, who paused just long enough for the tension to rise. Then, showing no emotion, he moved towards the young man, grabbed his hair in one hand and the seat of his trousers in the other. He lifted him clear off the ground and made towards the exit.

Astonished, the young man made no sound. Two members of Jackie's security team – one either side of the heavy double doors – solemnly opened them as Jackie approached. Once outside, Jackie dropped the young man onto the gravel, then turned and walked slowly back to the casino. All eyes were on him.

He smiled. 'It is now,' he said. Everyone relaxed, conversation continued, drinks were drunk, wheels were spun.

The member who had brought the young man, apologised.

'I think perhaps you should return him to where you found him,' Jackie said. 'He is far too excitable to be allowed out. He needs something to quieten him; tell him to take up embroidery, abroad.'

Unable to determine from his demeanour if Jackie was serious or joking, the man apologised again and left. However, the incident only seemed to underline what Jackie had been thinking for some time. The young man had struck a nerve. *Would I*, Jackie thought, *be welcomed at such a place as this if I didn't own it?*

CHAPTER THIRTEEN

A short time after the episode with the young man, an incident occurred that proved to Jackie what he had long believed about himself. He had all the girls he could wish for, more money than he could possibly need, all his businesses were a success, and 'Laughtons' was to be the pinnacle of his achievements. What he really craved, though, was power; covert power; power that he could exercise from the shadows. He wanted to control people, to control events themselves, totally. The only question that remained was how to satisfy this craving. He thought he had the answer, and decided to put it to the test.

The composition of the board of directors of 'Laughtons' ensured that the membership would be made up of their associates, their friends, and their acquaintances – almost all of them powerful people in influential positions. The very people who thought of themselves as not being under the constraints imposed on ordinary people. They thought they could get away with anything – and usually they could. All thought they belonged to a unique clique who took care of each other.

Then there were those who knew this to be a fallacy – one of whom was the Chief Whip of the ruling party of government. Made aware that many MPs, junior and senior Ministers, and leading lights in the civil service had been drawn to 'Laughtons', he paid the club a visit. A coarse, crude man, to whom subtlety was a word missing from his vocabulary, he was used to bullying and frightening those he held sway over.

He sought out Jackie and came straight to the point. 'I'm told you are a firm believer in discretion and, more importantly, a man of his word who can be trusted.'

Unaware of how to respond, Jackie chose not to.

The Chief Whip continued, 'A great many of my people come to your club, and I suppose spend a lot of money here because they can rely on you to ensure that any peculiar silliness they may display, and any peculiar difficulties in which they might find themselves, will invariably be dealt with satisfactorily by you.'

As Jackie had expected, a threat followed the praise.

'Of course,' the man went on, 'I can immediately stop all of them from coming here.' Seeing this had no effect, he softened his approach. 'But why should I? They might find themselves in the same sort of trouble in a place that doesn't have a Jackie to hold their hands. I would like us to come to an arrangement. Keep my people out of trouble and keep me informed, and I will keep sending a lot of people with a lot of money to "Laughtons".'

Jackie smiled. 'I believe,' he said, 'that we speak the same language.' Then he asked, 'Will you join me in a drink? I have an excellent brandy, or would you prefer champagne?'

The Chief Whip chose the brandy. As he had expected, when he left the club, a box of the finest brandy had been discreetly placed in the boot of his car.

Samuel Waller was a junior minister in the government, who hoped for better things. An ambitious ex-grammar school boy, he had married a plain woman, older than himself, who was the only daughter of a sitting Member of Parliament. It was not a happy union, only made bearable by his absenting himself from the family home for long periods. He was handsome in that rough way that appeals to a certain type of woman. A good speaker, amiable and friendly when the need arose, he had what his supporters called, 'the common touch'. His detractors in his own party, however, who were in the majority, merely thought him common. He had made a considerable nuisance of himself until selected to contest an un-winnable seat and confounded everyone by winning it. His success and his rapid rise to junior minister was in no small part the result of a fevered campaign on his behalf by certain popular newspapers, who now claimed him as their own.

Although he had his strengths – some of them admirable – it was his weaknesses that first attracted the newspapers to his corner. Always willing to hedge their bets, they prepared for both his rise, in which they would actively participate, and for his fall which, should the need arise, they would gleefully facilitate. They knew that the English liked nothing better over their Sunday morning breakfast than to read of a spectacular rise that had culminated in an equally spectacular fall, especially if their victim's predilections had proven sufficiently distasteful to warrant loud condemnation from the pulpit. Unless, of course, the victim being pilloried was himself a frequent occupier of the pulpit, then his sins would be Hail Mary'd away, and he would be awayed to a new parish. These newspapers were aware that the national sport of the English, along with hypocrisy, was the bringing down of those they had raised.

An unlovable man away from the spotlight, Samuel shone in its glare. He was, he liked to say often, 'a man of the people'. He exuded the only quality needed in his profession to succeed: he was popular. He knew all of the right people and blended seamlessly into life at 'Laughtons'.

Jackie had accepted his application for membership at the request of the Chief Whip who, Jackie suspected, was no great admirer of Mr. Waller, and who asked Jackie to keep an eye on him. Jackie kept both eyes on him, because he realised he was himself being both used and tested.

Samuel was always accompanied by a large group of friends, who it was hoped would keep his indiscretions contained if not controlled. A group of young girls would arrive later and join his party, Jackie having quietly advised his security people to offer no resistance. Samuel, his closest friends, and a number of girls, took advantage – with Jackie's approval – of overnight stays. Infrequent at first, his visits soon became regular events, and when his longed-for promotion was announced, he threw a large party and caution to the wind. Jackie had been watching him and knew where his weaknesses lay. He made his own plans.

The promotion party grew louder and more raucous as the night went on. Senior Cabinet Ministers arrived in chauffeur-driven cars to slap him on the back and whisper their role in securing his promotion. Much wine was drunk, then the Cabinet Ministers were replaced by young girls who had almost dressed for the occasion. The first set of girls who had arrived had been met by Jackie, who paid them double what they had expected to leave quietly and remain quiet. To sweeten the pill, Jackie asked for their telephone numbers and promised them renewed business in the future. They left, purring. The second group of young girls knew what they had to do. Samuel and his friends were too drunk to notice that the girls they were expecting had been replaced, and didn't care; the new lot were young and beautiful and made them feel very important. Jackie, as always, hovered in the shadows.

It grew late, the restaurant and casino emptied, and the promotion party spilled out from their private room to gamble. Samuel, girls either side of him, scattered his chips at random and began to lose heavily. Egged on by the girls, most of whom were now only wearing their underclothes and balloons, he continued to play and to lose. Out of luck and out of cash, he asked for credit. Jackie nodded his agreement to the raised eyes of the croupier.

Elsewhere, Samuel's friends, caught up in the spirit of the occasion, abandoned their post. Each of them, with a semi-naked girl on their arm, drifted off into secluded spaces where champagne corks were popped and balloons were burst. Finally, bored and tired, Samuel made for his room, held upright by three girls. The croupiers and waitresses were allowed to leave, then Jackie issued instructions to his security team and retired for the night.

The next morning, as he left his room and made his way along the passage to the stairs leading down to the restaurant, he saw Samuel leave his room and walk briskly towards him. Jackie thought to himself that the man looked quite well, considering the drink and the girls, and whatever else.

'Good morning,' Jackie said. 'Everything all right?'

"Morning, Jackie. Yes, fine. Well, actually no. You see, I happened to invite a few girls to my room, just for a nightcap you know, and... well, the truth is they are still there and won't leave.'

'Are they OK?'

'One of them is still a little groggy. The other two are making... how can I say this... certain demands.'

'What sort of demands?'

'Money.'

'Pay them,' said Jackie abruptly, and attempted to walk on.

'Rather a lot of money, actually. You see, one of them – completely without my knowledge – brought in some drugs, which of course I never use, and I think one of the girls is possibly unconscious. And they say they know who I am. I think they may have taken some papers, documents, from my suit when I was asleep, and they are threatening to go to the newspapers.'

'How many are there?' asked Jackie.

'Three, maybe four, I think. I am not sure.'

'How old are they?' Jackie said, knowing the answer.

'Not very, I'm afraid,' replied Samuel.

'Yours might be the shortest cabinet promotion in the history of politics,' said Jackie.

'What can I do?' Samuel groaned, his face growing pale.

'Go down to the restaurant and order breakfast. By the way, where are your friends?'

'Still drunk,' Samuel replied. As instructed, he went down to breakfast.

Jackie knocked on the door of Samuel's room and walked in. The three girls, now dressed and presentable, were sitting on the edge of the bed.

'Good morning, girls.'

'Morning, Jackie.'

'How did it go?'

'Exactly as you said,' one of the girls told him. 'He was far too drunk to do or remember anything. These are for you.' She handed over Samuel's wallet, car keys, and address book.

Jackie reached inside his jacket pocket and took out three envelopes.

'As agreed,' he said, 'with a little bonus. I look forward to doing business with you again. Now, wait here until my chauffeur comes up for you. He'll take you where you want to go.'

Each girl stood up, kissed Jackie on the cheek, and thanked him.

'Until the next time,' they said.

'Until the next time,' Jackie answered with a smile.

He joined Samuel, who by now was deathly pale, his hands shaking as he drew heavily on his cigarette. His friends were sitting around him with bowed heads.

'I would like to speak to Samuel alone,' said Jackie. The friends protested, but Samuel waved them away.

'Samuel,' said Jackie, 'last night has proven to be very, very expensive for me. However, it could have proven even more expensive for you.'

'Could have?' asked Samuel.

'Could have,' confirmed Jackie.

'You mean—' Samuel began, but Jackie interrupted,

'On this occasion, I believe I have resolved the matter. You will hear no more about it.' Jackie smiled, 'These are yours, I believe.' He handed Samuel his wallet, car keys, and address book.

Samuel, almost in tears, whispered, 'Thank you, Jackie, thank you. I won't forget this.'

I know you won't, thought Jackie. *I'll see to it you don't.*

When Samuel and his friends left, Jackie returned to his office and made a telephone call. 'Ah, good morning Chief Whip, Jackie here. I thought you should know…'

The Chief Whip listened carefully, and when Jackie finished, he said, 'Thank you, Jackie, thank you. I won't forget this.'

I know you won't, thought Jackie. *I'll see to it you don't.*

True to his word, the Chief Whip ensured that membership and attendance at 'Laughtons' flourished.

Content with the outcome of the Samuel affair, but dissatisfied with his relationship with the Chief Whip, Jackie now sought to broaden his horizons of both power and influence. He had been made aware that some of his female employees had been asked out by club members. Usually, the informants were the girls themselves, seeking assurance that they would be allowed to do so and reassurance that it was safe to do so.

Jackie was pragmatic. All of his girls were very beautiful, none were naïve, and would obviously be drawn to the young, and not so young, rich men who frequented 'Laughtons' and in whom the girls could see a passport to a better life. However, they knew the inherent dangers and turned to Jackie for advice and guidance. He was prepared to offer both, at a price.

He knew the men in question, especially the young ones – those fresh out of university whose only knowledge of girls was limited to their own sisters and the sisters of their friends, girls that usually lacked a good education and were rather dull and unknowing, with absolutely no idea of what men wanted or desired. Jackie admired his girls greatly. They knew exactly what men wanted and exactly what men desired, and could supply both.

Jackie was happy to give his assurances and assistance, but he outlined his terms and conditions. No girl would see a club member without his permission. As any affair progressed, he would be given regular updates of what the man said or did. It was essential, he said, that the girls send passionate letters after first making a copy, received passionate letters in return, and that they handed them over to him. Should a girl actually find herself proposed to, and everything went ahead as planned, all letters would be returned and the matter never referred to again.

His girls readily agreed, all trusting Jackie implicitly. For his part, Jackie would guarantee the complete safety of the girls. The girls knew they themselves couldn't lose; at worst, they would be paid in triplicate for their efforts. First, their more than adequate salary; second, the money that was lavished on them by their admirers; and finally, by Jackie again for the information they gave him.

To his great relief, none of these girls ever mentioned the word love. Jackie's final instruction, which he demanded be adhered to, was that each girl kept a detailed diary. These would ensure that when the men tired of them – usually the older men tired, or families heard of and disapproved of them – a successful bargaining would ensure the girls were financially rewarded for their time. Any men whose predilections bordered on the exotic were outlawed; any man who threatened, frightened, or expected his girls to engage in any form of violence, found themselves on the receiving end of it. No girl was allowed to become a mistress in paid-for accommodation and still remain in Jackie's employ, and he went to great lengths to persuade all of his girls who thought of exercising this option not to do so.

The agreement worked perfectly, and Jackie quickly amassed a library of very explicit and passion-filled letters, which he read with amusement. What so-called love did to even the most cold fish of men never ceased to amaze him.

Before long it was Jackie who controlled the Chief Whip, and not vice versa. He became the one who could destroy a career, a marriage, or a reputation in a second. He could make people do exactly what he wanted them to do. He could intimate to those on the way up that he could speed their ascent – and did so. He could advise someone of the name of someone who wished to bring him down, and therefore have it avoided. He could ask for people to be placed in positions that would benefit him, and ask for people who held positions of no benefit to him, to be removed.

He now had both power and influence and was happy to abuse both, which he did with a vengeance.

He destroyed the careers or the marriages of anyone and everyone who he thought had slighted him. And he reserved his special contempt for any men who threw themselves at his feet begging for mercy, ensuring their pain and agony be exposed for all to see. To these men, he was vicious and cruel, slowly savouring the moment. Should a wife or a mistress intercede on behalf of a lover or a husband, he would agree to stay his hand, which he did, knowing all parties would then fall further under his control.

It was at this point he became aware that a new type of woman was attracted to him. Those strange creatures who he had often witnessed at the ringside at boxing matches, hoping the spilled blood or spraying sweat would wash over them. Those strange creatures who rode out with the hounds, determined to be present as the hounds ripped apart the fox, or brought down the stag. They, who at the point and at the moment of the kill, bit their bottom lip until it bled and believed themselves to be more alive than at any other time in their lives. Jackie and his methods excited them, and so they pursued him until, wishing to try any new experience, he allowed himself to be caught. He quickly came to realise, however, that neither he nor any other man could satisfy their needs.

Jackie's close observation of both MPs and the civil servants who for a long time made up the greater proportion of those visiting 'Laughtons', led him to the conclusion that his grandmother's opinion of the MPs, in particular, had been justified. It could be argued in their defence that Jackie was only able to judge them at their worst, watching their playing field antics, referring to each other by the nicknames given to them as children, and their high levels of naughtiness.

Left alone to find new ways of raising taxes or creating new laws, needed or not, they were a relatively harmless species. Only when they adopted 'a cause' did they become a nuisance to themselves, their colleagues, and more often than not, to the cause itself. Causes that were generally completely obscure, ensuring that their intervention only raised the levels of indifference and boredom previously attached to it. More often, though, they believed they had to pursue a 'great cause', ideally on foreign soil; some issue long dormant, but unpleasant to their senses, that they decreed must be resolved for the good of the indigenous population.

Usually, however, the inhabitants of the foreign soil in question were unaware of such unpleasantness and resented the intrusion. Invariably, therefore, the MP's intervention was interpreted as interference and rejected. If Britain had not already been banished from the foreign soil in question, banners would quickly appear, proclaiming 'Britain Out'. Bruised and bewildered, the MPs and their dwindling band of supporters would disappear never to be seen or heard of again.

The civil servants were a different breed – a closer, tight-knit community who, in contrast to the MPs they controlled, ran a marathon not a sprint. Chameleons called upon to change their colours every four years or so, they had to be, and were, permanently civil. They carried a pen in one hand, a sharpened knife in the other, and were expert at wielding both. They were the only true opposition to the ruling government, a role they had adopted unwillingly, but out of necessity, having too long witnessed that the officially elected opposition always failed in their duties. It was they alone who strove to ensure that those to whom they were expected to defer, concentrated on carrying out the duties they were elected to perform. The majority of their time and efforts, however, were devoted to protecting the MPs from themselves, and more importantly from their ambitions.

CHAPTER FOURTEEN

A highly influential High Court judge had made it his business to befriend Jackie. Whenever he visited 'Laughtons', he always made an effort to speak to him, and often the two of them would dine together. Although initially a little flattered, Jackie was also wary. But after a period of time, Jackie warmed to him, believing the judge harboured no sinister or corrupt intentions. The judge was a sad-eyed, kindly man who he said had witnessed too often the battlefield of conflict and confrontation that is the courtroom.

Once again, Jackie was surprised how the most powerful of men were apt to take him into their confidence. *Why*, he wondered, *did they feel a need to impress him?* For although he considered himself a good listener and sufficiently intelligent to hold a conversation with anyone, it was common knowledge that he shunned close contact. However, he didn't dwell too long on the subject. He enjoyed the man's company, and it did him no harm that others saw and remarked on their friendship. The judge liked a drink and Jackie happily supplied him with it.

Often the last to leave the restaurant, they would speak together into the early hours, the judge doing most of the talking. He spoke with undisguised horror of the bewigged, cruel-eyed assassins who hid behind their raven black gowns, who believed justice was a word to be held in contempt, and conspired to ensure truth died from neglect. These were the men, he said acidly, whose lust for money and advancement took precedence over any act of morality. These were the men who looked upon all who came before them as guilty until proven guilty. All, they considered to be weak and useless, who came begging them to return what their stupidity had caused them to lose.

'None,' the judge would say, 'display an ounce of compassion or understanding of the lives of those whose future they would happily destroy. All of them are highly educated fools, with no knowledge of real life. Most are bigger rogues than those they prosecute. They disgust me,' he would add bitterly. 'They disgust me.'

Time after time, after a little too much brandy, he would succumb to melancholy, speaking sadly of those who were put up before him, who he referred to as different. He spoke endlessly and movingly of how these people were ostracised, ridiculed, and sneered at, usually and with the greatest venom by those who were different themselves but exhibited their difference in private.

'In truth,' the judge concluded, staring into his brandy glass, 'in truth, Jackie, we are all different.'

The judge himself, Jackie concluded, was different; he was too kind and too humane to be a judge. And too weak.

It was some weeks later when the judge took Jackie to one side and asked if he would accept his young nephew as a member. He described him as someone with a friendly, outgoing personality, a little too trusting, and – his voice trailed away – rather confused.

George Arthur St John Spencer came from a noble family and had been educated at a fine public school before joining a cavalry regiment. He now held a senior position in a royal household. He was also by far the most beautiful young man Jackie had ever met. He was about twenty-two years old but looked younger. Tall, painfully thin, he prefaced everything he said with a smile so obviously genuine that he immediately won over everyone he met.

On the day of his enrolment, he surprised Jackie by asking if he could also enrol his sister, the judge having made no mention of such an eventuality. Jackie agreed to his request. Signing complete, Jackie asked George if he would join him for tea in the orangery – something he normally only did with those he highly favoured. He felt completely at ease in George's company, the conversation flowing backwards and forwards effortlessly.

Over tea, George related to Jackie his childhood days, which he said had been idyllic; his schooldays, in which he said much time had been spent in avoiding education; and his days in his regiment, which he said were difficult. His present position he described as perfect. Few sentences were allowed to pass without an injection of humour, most of which was directed at himself.

His cheerfulness and optimism proved infectious. He was perhaps the only man Jackie had met who he thought it would be impossible not to warm to. As he rose to leave, George stepped forward suddenly, took Jackie in his arms, and kissed him on the cheek, saying with complete sincerity, 'Thank you, Jackie. Thank you for being so kind to me.'

On his first and subsequent visits to 'Laughtons', George wore a bespoke dinner jacket with a white bow tie. A white silk handkerchief rested languidly in the top pocket of his jacket, and a white carnation was pinned to his lapel. His highly polished, handmade shoes were of black patent leather. He arrived alone, but he was not alone for long. He captivated everyone he spoke to, and soon found himself invited to join other members having a drink at the bar, though he drank little, or he was invited to join them in the restaurant.

Both the matronly wives of the club's elderly members and the young girlfriends of younger members in particular, found themselves drawn to him. Everyone knew instantly where George was in 'Laughtons', as laughter announced his presence. Even Jackie's waitresses and hostesses fell under his spell, not only because of his beauty but because of his unfailing kindness and consideration. Often, to his undisguised delight, the chef would be called from his kitchen to be congratulated on his cuisine.

George never gambled, but was the first to congratulate those who won or commiserate with those who had not. Women found themselves standing closer to him when speaking than they would normally do with their own husbands, touching his arm or holding his hand as they spoke. All laughed loudly at his jokes that were amusing without being cruel. He was a great success.

Georgina, George's sister, arrived for her first visit to 'Laughtons' exactly two weeks later. She wore a beautifully tailored, long, black sequinned dress that was split to the thigh. The neckline was high, and she wore three rows of white pearls. Lustrous, long black hair fell onto her shoulders, her make-up was subdued, her lips painted red. She wore small, diamond studs in her ears and a single diamond and ruby ring on her middle finger. She carried a small, black leather purse, embellished with mother of pearl. Her shoes were handmade and high-heeled, emphasising her stature. Her eyes sparkled and her smile was warm and friendly. She was stunningly beautiful.

As she slowly made her way into 'Laughtons', the heads of both men and women turned. A second later, they turned again; Georgina was George. Jackie stepped forward to greet her with a kiss and a welcome that he sensed might be needed; it was not. She had arrived alone, but she was not alone for long. She captivated everyone she spoke to and soon found herself invited to join other members for a drink, though she drank little, or was invited to join them in the restaurant. Both the elderly husbands of the club's members and the younger men in particular, found themselves drawn to her.

Everyone knew instinctively where Georgina was in 'Laughtons', as laughter announced her presence. Even Jackie's waitresses and hostesses fell under her spell, not only because of her beauty but because of her unfailing kindness and consideration. Often, to his undisguised delight, the chef would be called from the kitchen to be congratulated on his cuisine. She never gambled but was the first to congratulate those who won or commiserate with those who had not. Men found themselves standing closer to her when speaking than they would normally do with their own wives, touching her arm or holding her hand as they spoke. All laughed loudly at her jokes that were amusing without being cruel. She was a great success.

This monthly pattern continued: once every two weeks George; two weeks later Georgina. Only when the royal household was on a foreign visit was this routine disrupted.

Jackie noticed that the happiest nights at 'Laughtons', were when George or his sister were in attendance.

It was two or three months later when Jackie noticed that the High Court judge and his wife were walking towards him. Without speaking, his wife took Jackie in her arms and kissed him, then the judge took Jackie's outstretched hand between both of his.

'Thank you, Jackie,' his wife said, her eyes full of tears. 'Thank you for showing such kindness to my nephew. Remember, Jackie,' she said in hushed tones, 'even the smallest act of kindness is never forgotten.'

No-one, however, stood out more in Jackie's memory than Alistair McDougall and his friend. Alistair was a Glaswegian Member of Parliament whose face still bore the scars of an ex-prize-fighter, which in fact he had been as a young man, and cheeks the colour of a whisky lover, which he still was. Short, with skin the colour of milk, little tufts of hair at the base of his neck, which had been dyed black – badly – and when in the House, wore suits of heavy Hebridean tweed. His shirts had once been white, and his knotted woollen tie was always pulled slightly to one side. When relaxing from his duties representing his Glaswegian constituents, which was often, he favoured the wearing of open-necked Hawaiian shirts and Rupert Bear trousers. When the drink had the better of him, he regressed to his native guttural tones, which only he understood. And which caused much consternation to the croupiers when he threw his chips on the table with instructions where they were to be placed.

His appearances at 'Laughtons' became legend. There was no strict dress code, as Jackie believed that the status of his membership and the muted elegance of his club would be sufficient deterrent to those who may have wished to be less formal. Exceptions were made for what was perceived as genuine English eccentricity, or in Alistair's case, Scottish. Summer or winter, the little Scotsman would arrive in a heavy, black Crombie overcoat, which he declined to give up, a long, flowing tartan scarf, a homburg hat, and brown open-toed sandals. He refused to wear socks on the grounds that socks were for 'kiddies and wimmin'. Although his eyesight was poor, hence his inability to place his own chips on the roulette table, he refused to wear spectacles. His wife, who few had ever seen, remained in Glaswegian exile.

On his visits to 'Laughtons', he was always accompanied by a giant Negress who, he claimed, he had rescued from a travelling circus, and who placed a comforting arm around his shoulders. Summer and winter, she wore a full-length mink coat that barely concealed her green wellington boots. It is not known if she wore socks. Tight black curls peeped below a bright red and yellow turban that she wore high on her head. No finger or thumb remained ring-less. Her smile was wide and warm, her teeth – except for the front two, which were missing – were perfectly white, her generously proportioned lips were blood red. Strings of coloured beads hung from her elongated lobes. She carried a *pince-nez*.

After too much wine, she was inclined to weep softly, lisping to Alistair, 'You never tell me you love me.' She called him Shooboo; he called her Momma. Only one small cloud of Glaswegian steeliness hung over the colourful couple; Alistair was a kleptomaniac. Small items – salt cellars, ashtrays, napkin holders, cutlery – disappeared into the darkened recesses of his great, black Crombie with disconcerting regularity.

Jackie instructed his security team to turn a blind eye. This predilection, however, became more serious at the gaming tables when, amid the bustle and confusion, as anxious players reached across each other to place their bets, Alistair believed it to be acceptable, when all his chips had been lost, to help himself to the chips of those gambling either side of him. When this occurred, Jackie gently asked Alistair if he and his lady would kindly give their expert opinion on a new malt whisky he had recently acquired. His security team would ensure that those who had lost their chips, without knowing they had lost them, had them discreetly returned.

Throughout the winter months, after eating, drinking, and gambling, they would repair to the most secluded corner of the club, where Momma would sit in a deep, leather armchair with Shooboo on her lap. The fur coat would be opened, and she would draw him close to her and rest his head on her chest. The fur coat would then be drawn around the two of them, and she would begin to slowly rock backwards and forwards.

On spring and early summer evenings, they would find refuge in the orangery or beneath the two trees.

Jackie had a great affection for them both.

Although George, Georgina, Shooboo, and Momma were the major players in the drama of 'Laughtons', mention should also be made of the spear-carriers

– those highly superstitious gamblers who believed that only they themselves held the magic key to winning.

There was the lonely man; someone who held a senior position in the government's accounts division, who, after feasting in the restaurant, would spend an hour scribbling down the sequence of numbers thrown up by the roulette wheel, before finally placing a small bet on a number that always failed to reward his efforts.

There was the Chinese businessman who only arrived at 'Laughtons' at 7.45pm, made directly for the roulette table, and at exactly 8pm placed a large bet on number eight. Win or lose, he would then return to his waiting Rolls Royce and be driven away.

There was the small, bald, bespectacled man with the Hitler moustache, who arrived at 'Laughtons' arm-in-arm with a tall German diplomat, who persisted in shouting out in a strong Bavarian accent, 'Broken biscuits', just before the ivory ball dropped into the bowl of the roulette wheel.

There was the man who, when he had a win – no matter how small – would shout out, 'Lamb for tea, lamb for tea.' Surprisingly, none of their fellow gamblers offered up any complaints about these outbursts, each secretly, but quietly, exercising his own 'good luck' method of beating the wheel.

These, and many others, were the characters that gave laughter and colour to 'Laughtons'.

However, 'Laughtons' was not all about strange characters, cold, hard business, or ambition or manipulation, or even about the simmering passions so often openly displayed, or of the ugliness of human nature. There were many long, hot summer days when

Jackie was content to wander alone through Lady Laughton's garden, now in its finest summer dress, or sip tea, alone but content, in the orangery. On these occasions, no lady was allowed to accompany him. In the garden and in the orangery, he thought only of Suzanne.

CHAPTER FIFTEEN

After Suzanne, and the successful launch of 'Laughtons', Jackie had to decide what to do. He wasn't a man given to introspection. It had never been necessary. He had always been supremely confident that what was meant to be for him would prove to be what he himself wanted. If for a moment he had doubted – and the photograph from Suzanne had caused him to doubt – it was only for a moment. The decision he had to make, therefore, was relatively simple: to change, or to carry on as before.

He could not change; he would not change; he would carry on as before.

The time of the year was rapidly approaching when he would escape the cruelty of an English winter for his Mediterranean farmhouse, but he thought he deserved a little relaxation before doing so. He was confident that he could leave the running of 'Laughtons' in the safe hands of his directors and his staff, all of whom shared and understood his passion for discretion. The rest of his businesses were being ably run by his managers. His social life became frenetic: too many parties, too many late nights, too many women.

Even during the opening of 'Laughtons', he had still kept in touch with and entertained half a dozen or so of the women he had known, especially those whose hearts still ached for him, those who would instantly drop whatever they were doing and whoever they were doing it with, to be with him. All of them hoped that this time it would be different, that it would last. The wiser heads among them simply enjoyed the moment, because they knew that it would not. But the women who refused to believe Jackie when he told them the truth – and he always told them the truth – were always in the majority. Those women who thought they were different, that they alone could change him, they were not and they could not, so they would be forced to withdraw, their hearts broken anew.

There were also those of a less sensitive nature who could tell a different tale. Unlike the majority of men they had met, no woman could ever accuse Jackie of being deceitful. From the outset, whether he sought out a woman, or a woman sought him out, he made it clear in a kind and gentle way that he was neither looking for love nor had any to give, and their relationship, should she agree to one, would last for not more than a month or two. Afterwards, he always said, he hoped they would remain friends. They would be assured that he would never discuss their time together. All of this would be conveyed to them quietly and with a warm smile. He would ask nothing of them, he'd say, that they were not prepared to give. They gave.

They would stay in the smartest hotels in great cities, or fashionable seaside resorts, their suite furnished with antiques and Old Masters. On a long, low table set in front of a *chaise longue*, upholstered in aged tapestry, would stand a crystal vase full of fresh roses, carnations, and lilies. At the side of the table in an ice bucket, there would be an open bottle of champagne, which, when the last drop had been poured, would be mysteriously replaced with another. She would be cosseted, and protected, and convinced she was the most beautiful and intelligent woman in the world. She would receive gifts of expensive scent, and jewellery so perfect it would take her breath away. Doors would be opened for her; she would be shown to the best tables in the best restaurants and fawned over by all who Jackie introduced her to. They would go to the ballet, to the opera, and to art galleries where Jackie would explain to her how beautiful things could be and how to understand and enjoy them. He was the perfect gentleman, and she was made to feel the perfect lady.

Then it would end.

Usually with a gift, always with a kind word.

And she would die a little.

Not everyone thought Jackie's behaviour acceptable. Sometimes, after the latest goodbye, small groups of men would appear at Jackie's office – brothers, fathers, uncles, boyfriends, who had met in a nearby public house and over drinks decided what they would do to Jackie. Replete with Dutch courage, they would arrive with a plan, which usually consisted of two or three of them holding Jackie while a fourth would give him the beating he deserved. They would turn up at Jackie's office to be met by his secretary and a security manager. They would politely be asked to wait, given tea, and informed that Jackie was in a meeting. Sufficient time would be allowed to elapse for the Dutch courage to abate. Then Jackie would invite them into his office, where they would be shown to their seats in front of his desk, but spaced apart. Jackie would stand in front of them. Sobered and disadvantaged, they would splutter out their grievances. Jackie would listen patiently, and when they had finished, begin his well-practised speech.

It was always at the point where he emphasised that he was doing nothing behind anyone's back, nothing deceitful, unlike those who had girlfriends on the side, had mistresses tucked away, or were cheating on their wives, that he'd see the eyes of his protagonists drop, and he would know he had them beaten. They left quietly to return to the same public house, another round of drinks, and a different conversation.

Only once had Jackie met his match.

A pleasant young man, who had put on an ill-fitting suit for a pre-arranged meeting with Jackie, and who had arrived directly from his place of work, calmly and politely, without any raising of his voice, explained the devastating effect Jackie's relationship with his twenty-year-old sister had had on her and her family. He explained to Jackie that she was an intelligent, and yes, a beautiful girl, who had never had a boyfriend and who had led a life of quietude in the care of her loving family. He admitted she was a dreamer and that Jackie had made it clear that the relationship would be temporary. He spoke about his sister lovingly, ashamed that he had been unable to protect her.

Jackie listened in silence as the brother spoke of the pain being felt by his family. At last, if only to stop the flow of anguish, Jackie interrupted, 'I honestly thought she had had boyfriends before.'

The brother looked at Jackie for a long, silent moment. 'She hadn't,' he said. 'But you are not a boy.'

He stood up to leave. At the door, he turned to Jackie and said, almost in a whisper, 'My sister said you lifted her up so she could touch the stars, then you let her fall.'

When he had left, Jackie went to a mirror, checked his teeth were clean, and that he didn't need to shave. He applied the aftershave he always wore, and set off to meet the young woman he would be entertaining that evening.

He arrived at his Mediterranean farmhouse in early December to warming winter sunshine during the day and log fires and the local wine at night.

He returned in the first week of February to snow piled high against the roadside, icicles hanging from the eaves of roofs and windowsills, and new ideas for his business.

He had retained the services of the solicitors engaged by his grandmother, primarily because they knew far more about his various businesses than him, and because his grandmother would not have continued with them unless her faith in their ability had been complete. He had also developed a close working relationship with old Mr. Simpson's son, Donald, who had been instrumental in the successful opening of 'Laughtons'. The two men could not have had more different backgrounds, but each believed the other to be the more fortunate.

He had also decided to engage the services of a firm of solicitors who, although long established, had a young, ambitious team that specialised in specific business areas which Jackie believed might be of use to him in the future. He advised Mr. Simpson of his decision. Jackie always believed himself to be apolitical, although his first major decision after the opening and the success of 'Laughtons' could have been, and indeed was, seen as verging on the brink of socialism.

For his part, he believed his decision made good business sense, and therefore good money sense. He accepted, though, that his proposals were radical and, if not handled with great care, could prove to be most costly. He would, Jackie announced, dispose of all his shops and cafes – some 85 in total. Both Donald and old Mr. Simpson were appalled when Jackie suggested his idea to them.

Putting that number of businesses for sale, all at once, might indicate that they were losing money, severely depressing their value and all the other businesses remaining in Jackie's portfolio. Morale, he was told, would plummet. Jackie's solution, however, astounded them. The people presently running these businesses would be given the opportunity to purchase them. A price would be agreed, and terms arranged for the business to be bought over a three-to-four-year period. No-one knew the true value of these shops better than the people who ran them, he explained. Jackie would retain the freeholds, and each shop owner given a lengthy lease. Everyone would benefit. Jackie would benefit the most. He made it clear the proceeds would be used to invest in those businesses that remained. The managers of these remaining businesses, sensing an opportunity in the future, would take greater care of them as a result.

The proposal proved a stunning success. Jackie was surprised and a little alarmed at how quickly the money to purchase outright was raised. Once again, his grandmother had been proven correct in her understanding of human nature. As a consequence, Jackie vowed that any businesses he was to purchase in the future would only be those that employed the fewest number of people required to secure the greatest return of revenue. The problem with all businesses, Jackie knew, was not the weakness of the business but the honesty of the people running them.

If Jackie's proposals regarding the disposal of his shops was radical, his next proposal provoked disbelief and outrage. He intended, he said, to quadruple his stock of rented accommodation within two years. His method, he said, exuding confidence, was simplicity itself. He would purchase the freehold of run-down, neglected, but structurally sound Victorian terraced houses. He would seek an above average rent for these properties, but would first enter into an agreement with his potential tenants that any money they chose to invest in improving the property would be reimbursed by fifty per cent. There would be no rent increase in any year that they invested a certain amount of money, and no rent increase for three years after both parties had agreed the property to be 'finished'. Only those prepared to accept these terms would be considered.

'Madness,' was the verdict of other landlords.

Jackie charged Donald Simpson with helping him to make his proposal a success, while he himself produced the advertisements to launch the scheme. Within three months, he had a waiting list of over 250 potential tenants anxious to participate. Only then did he tell Donald that he had, during the course of the previous two years, purchased 175 run-down properties. Both of these initiatives, and the way he operated 'Laughtons', made Jackie's name in the business community. Through Donald, he joined a number of highly respected business and social clubs.

Within five years, Jackie was among that elite group of landlords who controlled in excess of 500 properties. The value of those originally purchased for next to nothing had since increased fourfold. Whole streets became respectable and desirable almost overnight.

It was exactly ten years after Suzanne that he received the first of many premonitions that major changes were about to occur in his life. The year indicated was only two years away!

He set about making plans.

CHAPTER SIXTEEN

It all began innocently enough at one of those dinner parties given for no particular reason, and attended by those who had nothing better to do. He had nothing better to do; ennui engulfed him.

The host and hostess were successful business people who thought such events elevated them in the thoughts of their peers. At such events, formality – initially at least – prevailed, for those invited to such events liked to think of themselves as both civilised and civilising.

Alcohol soon put a stop to such pretensions.

The last of the food, which had succeeded in its attempt at blandness, was being cleared away when a slightly tipsy, middle-aged woman, wearing a dress that would have looked better on someone younger, leaned toward him and asked a little too loudly, 'Is it true, Jackie, that you can see into the future?'

All other conversation ceased, and all eyes were suddenly directed at him, for she had asked the question everyone else would liked to have asked but lacked the nerve to do so.

Looking across at the girl, who was sipping from a flute of champagne, he answered, 'A lot of people seem to think so.'

In fact, he had no idea what people thought on the matter, but he relished any opportunity to relieve the triviality of the evening. A pause ensued, causing the other guests to move uncomfortably in their chairs and reach for their glasses.

'Must be handy at the roulette wheel?" joked a portly colonel, relieving the tension. He was a man for whom there couldn't be enough dinner parties of this nature, and was one who could always be relied upon to bring a little light relief to almost any situation. He was a man who held unshakeable opinions on everything of no importance, opinions he thought it his duty to share with the readers of certain national newspapers, who believed any letter signed and suffixed with (retd), afforded the letter a certain gravitas.

'I wouldn't know,' Jackie replied. 'You see, I don't gamble.' This was perfectly true. No-one seriously involved in gambling, as Jackie was, ever gambled themselves.

Someone said, they thought amusingly, 'Do you have a crystal ball covered over by a ruby red, star-emblazed, velvet cloth?'

'Or are you able to read one's destiny from a pack of playing cards?' intoned another.

'More importantly,' began a lady of a certain age, whose cleavage was on open display purely to distract from her equine face, and succeeded in doing so. 'More importantly,' she carried on, with a sly wink of the eye, 'do you give private readings?'

Everyone laughed. He shared the joke. As the laughter died away, he leaned over the table and in a loud whisper replied, 'Normally, no, but in your case, I would make an exception.' He fixed her with a gaze and smiled. For a second, she blushed.

'What about shares, Jackie?' said the business-minded hostess. 'What are you dabbling in at the moment?'

His immediate thought was to answer that he never 'dabbled' in anything, but instead he replied, 'I've told you, I don't gamble.'

Sensing their disappointment and seeing an opportunity to further the aura of mystery he wished to surround himself with, he said loudly, 'However…' and then paused.

He remembered a medium-sized, long established family business that had supplied one of his factories for many years. Old-fashioned in the extreme, the two brothers who now controlled the business were still referred to as Mr. David and Mr. Paul by their devoted and aged employees. They were a quoted public company with massive assets, no debt, and even less ambition. Jackie knew all of this because the fifth-generation son, Mr. David, had happily disclosed the information to him at a dinner party just like this one, only a few months previously.

'However,' Jackie went on, 'I do not, as you call it, dabble, but if I did, Darbyshire and Sons might be worth watching.'

It was exactly four days later.

As always, Jackie arrived at his office at 7am, his secretary at 6.30am. This gave her ample time to prepare his tea and toast and to lay out on his desk two morning newspapers – one financial, one popular. The raised cup was halted halfway to his lips. His eyes had caught a headline close to the bottom of the page of the financial paper.

SHARES IN DARBYSHIRE AND SONS SOAR, it blazed. The article explained how shares in this company had risen seven-fold in a little over 48 hours due to massive buying, first by private individuals, and later by large institutions. The owners of the business said they could give no reason why the shares had risen. Pressed further by cynical journalists, they emphasised that no take-over talks were being held. They stressed this point so well that everyone concluded that takeover talks were being held, causing the shares to rise even higher.

The author of the piece, a man with the title of Chief Analyst and Head of Projection, was clearly peeved that he'd had no prior knowledge that such a takeover was in the offing, and worse, had no knowledge of this company. Loudly proclaiming that such companies as this – 'docile sheep' companies, as he was to now, and later, refer to them – could no longer survive 'the modern world' of business. From this day forward, the wolves would be in pursuit of such sheep, was his confident prediction.

Jackie read the article over and over. *Could it possibly have been caused by the nonsense he spouted after too much champagne at that gruesome little dinner party?* For a moment, excitement gripped him; this was the sort of power that everyone aspired to. Power without responsibility. If the fools wanted to believe he could see into the future and select shares that would soar in price, then let them believe it. Whatever Suzanne could do... he pondered. Then caution set in.

Suzanne chastened, disenchanted, and rather disgusted with herself, had for a long time, he had been told, been a recluse. *Well,* he thought cynically, *she could now afford to exercise her newly-minted morality.*

He thought very carefully where all this could lead and decided it best be left alone.

But it was too late.

It would not be left alone.

All that day, his phone never stopped ringing. Everyone at the party had, they said, bought shares as he had told them to, and made a killing. Others rang to say they had bought the shares on the advice of someone who had been at the party, where they said he had insisted they buy these shares.

No-one thanked him. All presumed he had done very well out of it himself. He had not. He had never bought a share of anything in his life. Invitations flooded in. Everyone wanted to meet him; strangers introduced themselves to him in restaurants. Restaurant owners reserved their best table for him. The bill was always paid by some fellow diner, who also sent over a bottle of champagne and his business card. At his various clubs, members who previously had never even acknowledged him, became friendly, offering to buy him a drink or asking him to accompany them in a round of golf – a game he had never played. Over the next few weeks Jackie's name was attributed to each and every share that rose in price.

A friend of a friend of Jackie's, it was said, had it on good authority that such and such a share was the next to be targeted. Obviously, the man himself couldn't be expected to comment publicly, but... Jackie seemed helpless to prevent any of this. Outright denials of any involvement led only to a knowing wink and further buying.

Meanwhile, Darbyshire and Sons was taken over. Within weeks, all 150 members of staff, the family, and the board of directors were punch-drunk, battered, bewildered, and out of work. Farmland and buildings and factories were sold off. Within two months, the business did not exist.

Jackie maintained a low profile, refusing all invitations, retreating more and more into himself.

His first venture out – some six months after the Darbyshire destruction – was a visit to one of his clubs for lunch. As he entered, he saw sitting morosely in a corner, staring blankly out onto the pavement, David Darbyshire. He was nursing a brandy. He looked up, saw Jackie, and walked over to him. Without a word, he threw the contents of the glass into Jackie's face, put down his glass and left. Aware that everyone was looking at him, Jackie slowly removed the handkerchief from his top pocket and mopped his face.

Theatrically, he began licking his lips and said, 'The amount of money I am credited with making for him, you would have thought he could at least afford a decent brandy.'

Everyone laughed and raised their glasses to him. Inwardly, though, he seethed. Not for the first time, he was making a great deal of money for others, if only by default. And he knew that the more he made for them, the more they resented him.

He felt responsible for the destruction of a company that had further enriched them, and derived no pleasure from it. In fact, he felt ashamed of himself. Everyone was careful to be friendly to his face, but behind his back he knew of the list of sobriquets now being attributed to him. The most popular, since the opening of his casino, was 'Black Jack'.

The resentment was felt most keenly by those financial journalists who had, in their opinion, been made to look foolish and incompetent. Equally, there was no shortage of people ready to sympathise with them. Collectively, they determined to destroy him. However, such was the depth of their detestation, their blindness in pursuit of revenge – all fuelled by their intake of drink – that they made error after error.

The first was in allowing Jackie to discover their intention. Having declared from the outset of what came to be known as 'The Darbyshire Saga', that the 'docile sheep' were ripe for ravaging, they had to make good their predictions. A list of those businesses that would be the first to be consumed was produced, with in-depth analysis and a recommendation to buy. Forewarned, however, those companies that harboured no desire to be sacrificed took steps to ensure that they would not be. Shares in these companies rose quickly after the journalists' recommendation, only to fall back just as quickly when no takeover materialised.

The market was flat, because this was July. The very few shares that did rise were attributed to Jackie's influence, and the more he denied any involvement, the less he was believed. Shares recommended by the journalists languished or fell. Investors lost money. Investors didn't become investors to lose money, and rather than blame themselves for what in fact was simply their greed, they sought to place the blame elsewhere – and these journalists were the easiest targets.

Large institutional investors, who had purchased on their recommendations, sought meetings with the newspaper proprietors, questioning their competence. They threatened to withdraw their advertising unless there were improvements. Readers, both rich and not so rich, complained on the letters' pages. Institutions and individuals alike voiced the same complaint. How could all of these professionals, with all their expertise and experience, with their fine education and so-called deep knowledge of their business, fail so miserably, fail so expensively, while, it was alleged, some private individual could be so successful.

The proprietors, anxious to appease all parties – especially as they were soon to embark on their annual summer holidays aboard their yachts in the south of France – initiated two well tried and tested solutions. First, they emphasised the point that their journalists, all men of incomparable honesty and character, had always made it clear to their readers that benefits accrue in the long term. This was where their expertise lay, the long term. This was where their in-depth analysis and deep knowledge was of most benefit; they were not purveyors of get rich quick schemes. Knowing such an explanation would not sufficiently appease all who had lost money, the proprietors then resorted to their second solution. They fired half a dozen journalists.

Jackie, in the meantime, had devised plans of his own. But first, aware of the inherent dangers of his scheme, he held lengthy meetings with his own solicitors and also with the independent firm he had engaged which had expertise in the understanding of the laws of slander and libel. Both firms were advised of the stated intentions of the journalists to destroy Jackie's reputation and, in doing so, his businesses. Both firms, excited by the large fees in prospect, expressed their sympathy for him and distaste for his detractors. Unbeknown to both sets of solicitors, Jackie had already hired two private detectives and briefed them of their duties. The names of ten of his most prominent adversaries were given, along with the instruction that everything it was possible to know about these people must be discovered.

'You will be paid a retainer,' Jackie explained, 'and all expenses will be reimbursed. Should you supply the irrefutable evidence I need, you will receive a substantial bonus. I can be very generous.'

With the tacit approval of Donald Simpson and his father, Jackie instructed them to secure the services of at least four retired senior ex-police officers, one of whom should be an ex-deputy chief constable, and all of whom must be of impeccable character and well versed in the working of the City of London Stock Markets. Their brief, Jackie stated, much to the surprise of the solicitors, was to investigate him. They would be given full access to him, all his businesses, all his personal, private, and business dealings. They must, Jackie declared in a tone that even surprised him, prove to his solicitors that neither he, nor anyone closely associated with him, had ever bought one single share in any company.

After this meeting, Donald took Jackie to one side, to urge caution. 'I am quite sure my father will engage the right people,' he said. 'Father is no fool, and the police can generally be relied upon to do a thorough job. It's only when they are investigating their own that they cannot be trusted. I would like you to remember something, Jackie,' he cautioned, 'and please don't think I am being patronising. I deal with the police almost every day and my conclusion is as follows – there are two types of what we refer to as the general public. The first type are those who have never had any dealings with the police. Their opinions are unshaken; the police, they believe, are a wonderful body of men dedicating themselves to assisting and protecting them, and who will be there to help them when they need help the most. The second type will have had dealings with the police. Their opinions have been shaken; they know the truth. And you, Jackie, belong to the first type, which is why I caution you.'

Privately, both sets of solicitors believed that Jackie was up to something.

He was up to something.

For a considerable time now, he had known that the next few years would be most eventful, and would bring about the biggest change to his life since that day on his fifteenth birthday when he had been given over to his grandmother. He had instinctively known that on that day, and also on the day he met Suzanne. And again now, he knew unseen forces were at work. Knowing this change was coming, he had sufficient time to prepare. So he prepared.

Suzanne had caused him to doubt. She had also discovered something deep inside that disturbed him. She had taught him he could feel. And then she'd betrayed him. But he could not, he dare not, accept that the instinct that had governed and controlled each hour of each working day had failed him. If he did so, what was left for him to believe in?

Since Suzanne, but not because of Suzanne, he had become more and more dissatisfied. His relationship with others had deteriorated to the point where he was as disgusted by himself as much as he was disgusted by them. That was his fault. He chose to live among them, to socialise and do business with them. He had also chosen to break his own rule of never seeking the limelight. In an effort to contradict the nonsense being gossiped about him, he had allowed himself to be interviewed by the financial journalists. Though he was charming and polite, he told them nothing. That didn't prevent them from concocting a story that just fell short of referring to him as a confidence trickster. Worse still, in an attempt to redress the balance, he had agreed to two separate meetings with two female journalists, and had convinced himself he would be able to persuade them to write something a little more flattering.

These interviews followed the same pattern as with the male journalists. The late-night dinners and hotel visits that took place after the interviews did not. All to no avail. Similar stories, much embellished with lurid personal details were told. Only this time, the final articles appeared not in the financial papers but in the women's section of the newspapers. None of the resultant publicity did him any harm, much to the annoyance of the journalists. In fact, their plan – for clearly, they had a plan – completely backfired. Readers wrote in suggesting he be given a weekly financial column of his own, and the women's feature editor received dozens of requests for photographs and an avalanche of requests for his phone number. Seeing a human-interest story, the popular press pursued him.

Not one to make the same mistake twice, Jackie refused all requests for interviews. As a consequence, invented, colourful articles appeared, given by 'a close friend' or someone 'wishing to put Jackie's side of the story'. All were spiteful; all were fiction. As each share recommended by the financial experts fell, and any share that rose was attributed to him, their hatred of him festered.

Jackie was seriously aggrieved, and he was never able to nurse a grievance for long.

He decided it was time to put a stop to it.

Jackie was confident of success. He had been around vacuous people for far too long – businessmen, politicians, journalists, and the gossip columnists. They only confirmed what he already knew. Men only wanted to know him because they believed he could make them rich.

Women only wanted 'to know him'.

He knew all of their weaknesses – prime among them being greed. Deceit came a close second, and came as easily as breathing. Deceit of their spouses first, then of their friends. Deceit, which they seemed only too happy to discuss loudly when drunk, to anyone who would listen. Jackie was a good listener. He had long ago perfected the art of appearing drunk, when in fact, he seldom was. For some reason, these people liked to think they were impressing him. They were not.

He reserved a special contempt for those just-a-little-too-old company directors, with their just-a-little-too-young mistresses, who saw no point in owning them if they couldn't show them off. And the showing off proved to be a very expensive exercise. These were the men who were always open to offers.

And there were always those ready to make offers to them. All believed themselves immune from exposure of either their private or business lives, because they knew they were all at it.

Having been sworn to secrecy, the ex-police officers set about their task with exemplary zeal. It was a matter of pride, they told each other. 'Jackie is up to something, he's too confident, too clever. We'll turn his businesses upside down until we find what it is.' But Jackie had no need to be confident or clever; there was nothing for them to find.

After an exhausting three weeks, they finally admitted as much. However, to their surprise and to the surprise of his solicitors, Jackie instructed them to re-check everything, look closer, look deeper. Now they were incensed. He was laughing at them. So they re-checked, looked closer, looked deeper. They still found nothing.

Their final report, proffered before any payment was given, was masterful. It explained in great length the details of their investigation, the number of documents scrutinised, the number of people interviewed, the time examining the share registers with experts. They concluded that there was no proof Jackie had ever purchased any shares at any time, or had any shares purchased on his behalf. They found that no monies from any of Jackie's companies had ever been diverted for this or any other cause.

Jackie's honesty and reputation was enhanced. His solicitors were delighted. The ex-police officers accepted both the agreed payment for their endeavours and the additional bonus, without demur. Four more men now despised him.

The two private detectives allowed no emotion to cloud their work; they were just as diligent, if not more so, for their motivation was, pure and simple, money. Jackie understood this. When confronted with page after page of their findings, he showed no surprise at the content or the relative ease with which they had secured the facts he wanted. All of his enemies had many enemies of their own. Jackie was amazed how indiscreet they had been, and how easily they had allowed themselves to be recorded and photographed in the most undignified of positions.

After carefully studying their report, he paid them, adding a bonus that raised their eyebrows. 'Now, gentlemen,' he said, 'time to earn some real money. Go back, look closer, look deeper. I want more explicit photographs, I want hotel receipts, I want witness statements. Give me what I want, and I will give you this.' He wrote a number on a piece of paper and showed it to them. Their mouths fell open.

After a slight pause Jackie added, 'Each.' He handed them another piece of paper. 'Here are the names of the six people I now want you to concentrate on.'

Whilst all this had been taking place, Jackie had been very busy himself. He re-launched himself onto the party scene. His timing was perfect. He had been told that the journalists, bitter at the sackings of their colleagues, were now even more determined to destroy him. In doing so, they had sought the assistance of their gossip columnist colleagues, who happily agreed to help them. Even Jackie conceded that fate seemed to be on his side, for that late July and August, there simply was no news of importance. No wars had broken out, no famines had struck the African continent, there were no rail disasters, no ships were lost at sea. No government minister was discovered in a compromising situation, and country vicars contrived to control their predilections.

Jackie was good copy. Jackie was the only copy. He attended all the social events of the summer. Each evening, he visited different restaurants with a different woman. In the early hours, he visited a nightclub or a casino, having first dispensed with the services of one woman, and where another woman would be waiting to greet him.

He constantly gave the impression of drinking too much and spending even more. His tips grew legend. Waiters fawned over him. He was heard to remark, 'There's plenty more where that came from.' And he made quite sure he was heard.

On the pretence that he was about to buy one, he borrowed a new Rolls-Royce for a week. At his clubs, he became expansive and sought out the loose-lipped to give his views on shares, and privately and discreetly agreed he was able to see into the future.

'It's the gypsy in me,' he would laugh.

He played a new game. Swaying a little, his champagne glass spilling over, he would say in the early hours to a small group encircling him, and who would be waiting patiently for this moment, 'I would not, I repeat, I would not buy shares in such and such a company.' This would be accompanied with a wink.

Within days, that companies shares soared. He also knew the gossip columnists normally employed people to feed them titbits they could use. Now they employed people just to concentrate on him. They were rather sad little individuals, who believed themselves to be embryonic journalists. They only drank when others bought, never ate in the restaurants, or gambled at the tables. Their only attribute was a capacity to laugh loudly at the cruellest of jokes. But they were a determined lot. So Jackie used them, reading in the following day's newspapers what they had reported, what he had told them he expected to see reported.

He had won them over; he had bought them over. They reported to him.

The gossip columnists stepped up their act of destruction. At first, things of no importance were reported – the restaurants, the girls, the clubs. Slowly, this changed. They resorted to using a string of sobriquets. Then they began naming Jackie, attempting humour to deflect from the bile.

'A certain exotic gentleman. A gentleman who could easily be taken for not being an Englishman. A gentleman with a penchant for vintage champagne and immature girls. A friendless gentleman buying friendship as easily as he buys shares.'

His evening and daytime activities were reported in full. Encouraged by the financial journalists, they stepped up the pressure. 'The gentleman known as "Black Jack". The popular predictor of the future who has recently acquired a new Rolls-Royce and seems to have money to burn, but whose money?' was finally followed by and almost in desperation, 'The gypsy gentleman's share dealings have once again enriched certain people in the know, as well as himself.'

It was at this point that both firms of solicitors wanted to act, but Jackie prevented them. He wanted more than an insincere apology tucked away in some corner of the paper. He wanted more than 'costs and damages', which he would be expected to donate to a charity of his choosing.

'Those who seek to destroy must themselves be destroyed,' he said. He knew the newspaper proprietors were ensconced on their yachts in the Mediterranean and couldn't easily be reached; he knew senior legal executives were absent. He knew that by doing nothing, he would embolden them. He was correct. The financial journalists and the gossip columnists believed Jackie dare not complain because he *did have something to hide*. All the time, the financial journalists were anxiously trying to gain proof of what he was hiding, consuming more and more alcohol as they failed to do so. No mention was made of the fact that the last four companies the newspapers had featured had seen their share price fall.

Jackie received a late-night phone call from the private detectives. They had been offered some very explicit photographs of a newspaper proprietor and his mistress. When they advised Jackie that the proprietor was Lord Eaton, and his mistress was the wife of one of the papers' senior financial journalists, Jackie's immediate response was to say, 'One, make sure they are absolutely genuine; two, buy them, regardless of cost.'

The recently ennobled Lord Eaton was a regular churchgoer, a family man, whose newspaper boasted the largest daily circulation in the country. And a man who regularly railed against the declining moral standards of the country; a man who had fully supported his chief financial journalist during and after the Darbyshire saga; a man whose financial journalists and gossip columnists were at the forefront of those who had sworn to destroy Jackie. When the private detectives met Jackie with the photos, they dropped a bombshell. Lord Eaton's mistress had purchased a large number of shares in Darbyshire and Sons.

The pictures themselves saddened him, not because he was a prude – he was not. Not because of the ugliness of the woman, or the gross hypocrisy of the proprietor.

But simply because both of them looked so desperately unhappy. *Also*, Jackie thought, *people of a certain age should never take all their clothes off and leave the lights on.*

Jackie enquired how the private detectives had come by the photos.

'It would appear that Lord Eaton's newspaper had been very hostile to a certain country, and he was using his influence to prevent certain trading agreements taking effect. I think that Lord Eaton's religion may also be a factor. The people who provided the information also told us that the country in question had acquired secret investments in Great Britain, extending to our finest hotels. However, when we checked the documents at Companies House, they clearly stated they were British-owned, and yet, having met and spoken with these people, I believe they do own these hotels. I should also tell you that we could only obtain these photographs, with the potential for gaining more, by giving an assurance that you would use them. I must also advise you that these people expect such assurances to be honoured."

The rest of the information Jackie sought came easily.

CHAPTER SEVENTEEN

Events moved swiftly. Jackie convened a meeting with both sets of solicitors and laid out the evidence he had gathered before them.

Most of the evidence.

That pertaining to Lord Eaton he did not.

Selective information concerning certain individuals he did not.

Jackie instructed his team on the strategy they would be pursuing. He also advised them that the solicitors whose forte was libel would be the lead team, and the senior member of his own solicitors, Donald Simpson, would be in attendance. Four national newspapers – two popular, two financial – two regional newspapers, and one magazine, would all be targeted.

He decided that they would meet with the legal representatives of the two regional newspapers first. The weight of the legal documents landing on their desk, and the reputation of Jackie's legal team, ensured a prompt reply. Called into the oak-panelled, austere offices of Jackie's solicitors, they arrived giving the impression – a false impression – of being contrite. Members of the opposing teams engaged in battle; their weapons dense points of law, their manner gentlemanly. For a quarter of an hour, Jackie watched, sipping his tea. Then he struck.

'Gentlemen, these are my terms. For your part,' he said, addressing his adversaries, 'you will print an apology to me on the front page of your newspapers. I have a copy of the apology here. Should you agree, all legal proceedings against you will be discontinued, and I will seek no redress – financial or otherwise. Refuse, and I will put the evidence you have been given before the courts. Of course, I cannot guarantee that the new evidence I have will not be made public before the trial begins.'

After a pause, Jackie went on, 'This industry is, as you know, beset with rumours. You have exactly thirty minutes to give me your answer.'

'This is highly irregular, and I must protest most—'

Jackie interrupted, 'Twenty-nine minutes.'

They were shown into a side room. After twenty minutes, they returned, insisting that certain alterations to the apology must be made and that they would only agree to its appearance on page five.

Jackie slowly lifted the crisp, white double cuff of his shirt to reveal his gold watch. 'Nine minutes,' he said.

They returned with a minute to spare, and agreed to Jackie's proposals in full. When they had left, Jackie's solicitors attempted to reprimand him.

He sighed. 'We are here to win, not debate. Those two regional newspapers will now print a front-page apology. Their speedy capitulation will give pause for thought to the bigger beasts, but they will not give in quite so easily. They will conclude, however, that an apology is all we require and decide not to take us too seriously.

'Gentlemen,' Jackie continued, trying and failing not to appear mocking, 'your schooling was of greater length than mine, your schools more august, your teachers well versed in the classics. So you will all have been taught the golden rule of all conflict: divide and rule.

'To proceed... the magazine. It is imperative you arrange a meeting for next Friday. Use the phrase you heard me use this morning, "to discuss new evidence that we have obtained, including distasteful indiscretions of your contributors" and emphasise "contributors". They will respond as we wish, through either fear or curiosity. Should they decline, however, make it clear that they won't be asked again.'

His solicitors were now absolutely convinced that Jackie was up to something, but two things prevented them from commenting. One, it was genuinely fascinating watching him, and two, their fees were accruing nicely.

The magazine was more of a comic than a magazine. It was popular among a certain class of reader who had yet to sever the umbilical cord of their childhood. Primarily, it was the plaything of a little group of would-be writers and contributors who would forego a fee to see their name in print. Its losses, which were substantial, were offset by the income from advertisements of a dubious nature, aimed at those of a dubious disposition, and by a declining number of benefactors who were able to use it to expose the more extreme peccadilloes of their enemies. In its heyday, now long gone, and more by good fortune than by good journalism, it had stumbled across a series of scoops that had resulted in the embarrassment of a number of people who should have known better, and a fewer number of people who deserved it, being imprisoned.

The meeting was arranged just as Jackie had demanded. In his usual highly meticulous way, he had commissioned a detailed report on all of those he considered may be a threat to him. The report concerning the editor of the magazine was comprehensive. He was, said the report, of small stock. A badly woven wig, which remained perfectly still even when his head moved, was seated on top of a cherubic face. A face which, when he had finished lecturing (he considered himself much too grand for normal conversation, having not the slightest interest in the views of others), assumed an expression that was a mixture of the whimsical and the smug. He was clothed in his father's hand-me-downs of cavalry twill trousers and a heather green Harris Tweed jacket, with leather patches at the elbow. His brown brogues were held together by years of caked polish, lace-less. His socks, odd in colour, were holed at the heels. To complete this affectation, he had adopted the habit of staring into the near distance, his legs crossed, his arms folded.

His solicitor – a grey, tired-looking man with the demeanour of one who feared that at any moment he might be struck off – showed Jackie, Donald Simpson, and Mr. Andrews into their office.

Having faced situations like this on numerous occasions, the editor and his solicitor were in no mood to be on the defensive, and they quickly made it clear that they were both dismissive of Jackie's impertinence at insisting on this meeting.

'Clearly, you are a most intolerable young man,' the editor said to Jackie, 'and clearly, your ego is greater than the sum of your achievements.'

Herewith begins the lecture, thought Jackie. He was right.

The editor continued. He saw no reason for anything they had published to be taken too seriously, no harm was intended, and no real damage done. 'Have you no understanding of the British sense of humour?' he murmured, slowly looking Jackie up and down, then down and up. 'No, I don't suppose you have.'

He went on to name all of those, far more famous than Jackie – politicians, lords of the realm, churchmen and, ending with a raising of the voice, royalty – who had taken what they had published in good part and without complaint. 'Remember,' he said, 'we have only repeated what far bigger beasts than us have printed.

'And to be honest,' he went on, 'we still have an awful lot of stuff we could publish, but as yet we have chosen not to.'

His veiled threat, Jackie thought, *was almost completely devoid of the veil.*

'And in all honesty, Jackie,' he said adopting that patronising tone much beloved by those who harbour no doubt of their superiority, 'do you really believe that by hounding us you will in any way enhance the reputation you appear to set such great store by? It will take at least a year before we get to court. A year for us, and others to—'

Like a country vicar too long at the pulpit being told to stop by a dowager duchess, Jackie cut in. 'Gentlemen, these are my terms.' He then repeated word for word what he had said to the regional newspaper proprietors, finishing with, 'You have exactly thirty minutes to give me your reply.'

They read the apology and smiled between themselves.

'We'll wait outside,' said Jackie.

He and his team stood outside the door; there were no chairs. After a moment, Jackie said, 'There is something I forgot to mention to them.' He walked towards the office door, knocked loudly, and walked in without being invited to do so. 'Sorry to disturb you,' he said.

'You're not disturbing us, Jackie, we have reached our decision.'

'I see,' said Jackie, 'but before you commit yourselves, could I ask, do you both agree that today is Friday, and it's the last Friday of the month?'

'If this is a joke, Jackie, do you mind if we use it in our next edition?'

'Not at all,' said Jackie, 'if you find it amusing. I believe that on the last Friday of the month, a certain amount of money finds its way into your bank from a benefactor who wishes to remain anonymous, and that this donation really is the difference between you staying in, or going out of business. A quick phone call will tell you if your bank has received the money today.'

The editor telephoned the bank. The answer was no. The manager was heard to ask if there was a problem, because if there was... The editor hastily put down the phone.

'As you rightly implied,' said Jackie, 'it could take up to a year before the matter gets to court. Do you really think you'll still be in business then? Especially when your bank – situated, I believe, at number 19 Westminster Place – and when the manager, I believe a rather dour individual name of McKenzie, is informed no further monies will be forthcoming from this source? I'll wait outside.'

Heated words could be heard emanating from the office, before Jackie and his team were called back in.

The editor made to lecture but was told to shut up. He shut up. 'We accept your terms,' said the solicitor.

As they left the office, Jackie noticed that the editor was staring into the near distance, his legs crossed, his arms folded.

It had not been difficult for Jackie to obtain the identity of the anonymous donor.

He was the anonymous donor.

In the days when the magazine was funny and eccentric, Jackie had been an admirer, always responding enthusiastically when donations were sought to ward off another threat of closure. Having no schooldays of his own, its silliness filled the empty gap where his childhood should have been. For too long now, though, the silliness had been replaced by that special sort of cruelty that only schoolboys can administer.

The apology was duly printed on the front page of the next edition.

The following month, having received no funds from the anonymous donor, the magazine began seeking donations from 'friends and supporters'.

Three months later, it closed.

Jackie reconvened a meeting with his dual team of solicitors. Once again, he outlined his strategy to them. 'We now have to deal with the four remaining national newspapers. All will have been in close contact with each other and those we have settled with. All will be bolstered by the fact we only wish to seek a quick solution and will be prepared to accept an apology and little, if any, compensation. Equally, all will present a combined front and instigate every delaying tactic in the book.'

'But isn't that what we want, Jackie, a quick solution?' his solicitor asked.

Jackie ignored this intervention. 'Our strategy will be as follows: we will concentrate solely on Lord Eaton's newspaper – the biggest, the most powerful, with an embarrassment of solicitors, QCs, and learned gentlemen at their disposal. Defeat the bad Lord Eaton and the game is won.'

'You make it sound remarkably easy,' said Mr. Simpson.

'It will be,' replied Jackie. 'It will be.'

'Jackie, I'm afraid I have to tell you,' said Mr. Andrews, firmly gripping the lapels of his finely tailored jacket, 'we are all becoming a little uncomfortable. We do not think you are telling us everything that we need to know, if we are to give you our advice and the correct legal guidance. To be quite blunt, Jackie, we think you are up to something, and we wish to make it clear to you that we cannot be party to anything untoward. Our reputations, you know.'

There followed a pause that seemed a great deal longer to them than it did to Jackie. He sighed a deep sigh; the sigh of a man whose feelings had been hurt. At least, that was what he hoped it sounded like.

'I believed,' he said with a pained expression, 'that by employing the services of the ex-police officers and giving them the brief that I gave them – with your full approval, may I add – and the results of that brief, that such a question would prove unnecessary.'

Embarrassed throat-clearing coughs and splutters followed this remark, but before they could add anything further Jackie continued.

'You have my assurance that nothing I do will give you any cause for concern. In fact, once this matter has been successfully concluded, I can guarantee that the reputation of both of your firms will be greatly enhanced. Yours will be the firms who took on the might of the British press and emerged triumphant.' This seemed to settle them a little.

'Now, to the matter in hand. These are my new instructions.' Turning to Mr. Andrews, he asked, 'What is the highest figure ever awarded by the courts in a case such as mine?'

As expected, Mr. Andrews reeled off from memory the case, the protagonists, the year, the court, and finally the size of the award.

'Thank you,' Jackie said. 'Now please contact Lord Eaton's legal boys and advise them that we will be seeking damages of exactly double that amount.'

Everyone in the room gasped. 'Jackie, Jackie, please listen to me,' pleaded Mr. Andrews. 'Even if you go to court, and even if you win, you will be awarded nothing like that amount.'

'As you quite rightly point out, Mr. Andrews, *if* we go to court. Make it clear also that we will attend no meetings where Lord Eaton isn't present. They will simply agree to meet us, then at the last minute, cancel and repeat the process time after time in order to frustrate us.'

'We simply cannot force them to meet us,' said Donald Simpson. 'As you have quite rightly pointed out, they have an excellent legal team at their disposal.'

'Correct,' said Jackie. 'That is why you will add a footnote stating that we have acquired new and significant evidence of a highly sensitive nature appertaining to the conduct and probity of senior executives in their employ, which we believe may be of interest to them.'

'And do we?' asked Mr. Andrews. 'Have we?'

Jackie was subsequently informed that although Lord Eaton had only recently returned from his summer vacation and had a tremendous workload to catch up with, he would consent as a matter of courtesy to the meeting. As requested, it would take place on September 7th.

The day prior to the meeting, Jackie cancelled it, due to a touch of influenza. No, he stated firmly when asked, the meeting could not go ahead in his absence.

A second meeting was arranged. This he also cancelled, this time without a reason being given. His legal team was exasperated, perplexed, and embarrassed, but said nothing.

Fortunately for them, it was Lord Eaton's team that had become increasingly anxious for the meeting to be held. They had been told that Lord Eaton had been informed that vicious rumours were circulating throughout the newspaper industry and among Lord Eaton's peers, concerning the content of certain new evidence. They were anxious that a meeting should urgently be arranged, so that such rumours may be quashed. Lord Eaton knew his enemies were legion and were only too happy to listen to these rumours, embellish them, and pass them on. Like all men who insisted they had nothing to hide, Lord Eaton had plenty to hide. If it was thought that Jackie was the instigator of these rumours – and it was thought so – no-one dare say so.

Eventually the meeting did take place in mid-November. At Lord Eaton's insistence, only he, his top legal advisor – a Mr. De Groote – Jackie, and Mr. Simpson would be at the meeting. They were met by Mr. De Groote – a tall, elegant, dapper man in his mid-forties – who led them through double mahogany doors into Lord Eaton's office overlooking the rising and falling of the bascules of Tower Bridge.

Large, framed maps of South Africa and aquatints of his ancestors, stern-looking, bearded men on horseback or leaning on long barrelled rifles, hung from the oak panelled walls. On his desk were bronze sculptures of leaping impala and charging elephants. Photographs of him, his children, and his grandchildren, littered one side of his desk. On the other side, facing into the room, were silver-framed photographs of Lord Eaton shaking hands with various prime ministers and leading business figures. One silver frame, larger than the rest, showed him in the ceremonial robes at his ennoblement.

One half of this vast, cold space was taken up by two green leather Chesterfield settees. Between them, on a small, oval, glass-topped table, was a vase of proteas.

Lord Eaton himself came as no surprise to Jackie, even though the two had never met.

Jackie reckoned he knew more about him than his own wife did. And the irony of this thought did not escape him.

Napoleon-short, with white, crew-cut hair, Lord Eaton had a round, ruddy farmer's face, which squatted directly onto his shoulders. He had no neck. His South African accent, which he made no attempt to disguise, was thick, guttural, and at times indecipherable. He was a bull of a man. (*After this meeting*, Jackie confidently thought, *he would be reduced to no more than a bullock.*)

If Jackie was not surprised by the appearance of Lord Eaton, Lord Eaton appeared almost speechless at the sight of Jackie. As Jackie walked towards him, his right arm outstretched in greeting, Lord Eaton just as quickly retreated with a look of horror and disgust on his face. *Clearly, Lord Eaton had not been fully briefed,* thought Jackie. Just as clearly, any carefully laid plans of how he would conduct this meeting were instantly abandoned. Cordialities were dispensed with. No tea was offered. *A shame*, Jackie thought, as he took his seat. He liked tea.

Lord Eaton had now retreated to his side of his gargantuan desk and eased himself into his high-backed, black leather swivel chair. He turned the chair to face the floor-to-ceiling window overlooking the Thames. He began in a low growl, 'I don't have time to waste on all of this nonsense. I have an important meeting in twenty minutes.' He turned in time to see Jackie slowly remove his watch and place it on the desk before him.

Lord Eaton breathed in deeply through his untrimmed nostrils, and continued, a slight increase to the growl evident. 'Your demands are ridiculous,' he said. 'I will pay no compensation to soothe your hurt pride. And as for an apology, I will simply say that this newspaper is not some silly schoolboy's magazine.'

'Or indeed some silly regional newspaper,' interjected Jackie.

'Or indeed, as you say, some silly regional newspaper. From what I have been told, we reported what you were up to and made it clear to our readers we didn't like it, or you.' He was getting more and more agitated. 'What do you suggest?' he asked. He was now on his feet leaning on his desk. 'You suggest we told lies about you and damaged what I can only laughingly describe as your reputation. Your reputation for what?'

His voice had now reached fever pitch; tiny beads of perspiration glistened on his forehead. 'Your reputation for lechery, for cavorting with girls half your age, for nightclubs, casinos, drunkenness, and I am told much, much worse. You are not a man, you're a conman.' He was out of control, unstoppable.

It was at this point, three or four minutes or so into this Lear-like rant, that Jackie suddenly realised what he was witnessing. Lord Eaton was not, he decided, the sort of man who would come to a meeting such as this unprepared. He would have done his homework, or at the very least had his homework done for him. He was not the sort of man who would suddenly lose all control of his emotions, even if he was confronted by a man who was the exact opposite of himself. And the implied racial element: too contrived, too convenient.

For although the rant was expertly enacted, all wild gesticulation and flying perspiration, the words aimed directly at Jackie were in fact controlled, stark, and menacing. Each sentence flowed effortlessly into the next, all the while increasing in intensity and power, each sentence ending with just the right degree of raised inflection. Each sentence delivering the same message: I am powerful, you are weak; you are nothing; I won't demean myself by mentioning your so-called new evidence, and by not doing so, devalue it.

Lord Eaton had chosen to believe what Jackie's solicitors had alluded to when asking for this meeting – misdemeanours of his senior staff, perhaps some high-end naughtiness of which he would have to publicly disapprove, embarrassment, nothing more than embarrassment. Lord Eaton was convinced that his darkest secrets remained secret.

Jackie concluded that this little play-let represented nothing more than a master class of bluff. His best course of action, he decided, was to sit back and enjoy the show. Just because he knew how the play ended, it should in no way lessen his enjoyment of the performance.

Lord Eaton had by now stormed around the desk to stand directly in front of Jackie. 'And you think you are going to sue me?'

He raged on.

Increasingly, Jackie couldn't understand what he was saying, as the rant disintegrated into a spew of coarseness and crudity. Little bubbles of spittle congregated at the corners of his mouth, his face bright red, his eyes popping. The rant continued unabated, mostly in a language that Jackie thought could only be Afrikaans.

Finally, a modicum of composure returned. Jabbing his podgy fingers into Jackie's chest, he said, 'Now let me tell you something. I didn't know at the time my people were after exposing your rottenness, or were determined to destroy you, but had I known, I would not only have supported them; I would have assisted them. You wouldn't be here today threatening me, you would be destroyed, you and all the filth like you who need to be destroyed. You have no idea how to behave, no idea of what being a gentleman is, but then again how could you possibly know?' He was almost calm now as he sat on the end of his desk facing Jackie. 'Where I come from,' he said, 'your kind would be lucky if my kind allowed you to clean our shoes.'

Jackie leaned forward. 'You still have six minutes, Lord Eaton.'

'I am done,' said Lord Eaton, 'and so are you.'

He returned to his seat, placed his short legs onto the desktop, crossed them at the ankle, put his hands behind his neck, and stared at the ceiling. Jackie noticed that the bottom of his shoes – that small space between the heel and the sole – had not been polished.

Lord Eaton, pointing a finger at Donald, said, 'Now you can go, and take that clown with you. De Groote, show them out.'

Mr. Simpson made to leave, but Jackie eased him back into his seat. Mr. De Groote stood, his apology ready to be delivered once they had left the office. Jackie bade him sit down too. Seeing the look on Jackie's face, he sat down.

'First things first,' said Jackie. 'Thank you so much for seeing me. I understand how very busy you must be. To be honest, I considered asking for a translation of many of your observations, however, I accept that nothing could be gained from doing so.'

Mr. De Groote knew what was coming next.

Donald knew what was coming next.

Lord Eaton, no fool, knew what was coming next. He had placed his cards on the table and knew it wasn't a winning hand. The fire that had raged within him, contrived or not, was extinguished.

Jackie reached down for his briefcase, his eyes fixed firmly on Lord Eaton. He opened the case, withdrew a large, brown paper envelope, and propelled it across the desk.

'This may be of interest to you,' he said.

Mr. De Groote reached across for it, but Lord Eaton was quicker. He withdrew from the envelope a sheaf of documents, and a dozen black and white photographs.

Whatever he had expected, he hadn't expected this. His face went grey and he seemed to shrink into his seat.

After what seemed an age, he said, 'Mr. De Groote will show you into an office where you can wait while we discuss this matter further.'

Jackie stood, put his watch back on his wrist, and said, 'No need. We're done.'

In the car on the way back to the office, Donald said, 'I thought you didn't gamble, Jackie? If Lord Eaton had called the police and accused you of blackmail, he almost certainly would have been granted anonymity, and time for his powerful and influential friends to do what such people do. And you would have gone to prison.'

'You are mistaken on two counts,' said Jackie. 'First, if you recall, I merely gave Lord Eaton an envelope containing documents and photographs, and the only words I spoke were, "These might be of interest to you." Had the police been called in, both you and Mr. De Groote would testify to that. I would have explained to the police that these documents had been sent to me, and as proof of my desire to resolve my differences with Lord Eaton, in a gentlemanly way, I had simply passed them to him. And the second count?' Jackie turned to face Donald and smiled. 'I knew what was in that envelope.'

His work complete, Jackie left the details to his legal team. Lord Eaton's advisors demanded certain assurances. The most important of them being that any copies of the document or photos be destroyed, and that the financial settlement between Jackie and Lord Eaton remain confidential. Jackie signed the documents, agreeing to both demands. The apology appeared on page one.

The proprietors of the three remaining newspapers, incredulous at Lord Eaton's capitulation, and terrified of what Jackie knew and what he would do next, panicked. Each printed the same apology on the front page of their newspapers before being asked to do so. Jackie received record amounts of compensation from all four national newspapers.

CHAPTER EIGHTEEN

Jackie waited patiently for two weeks for the situation to calm down before bringing the matter to a conclusion that would satisfy him. As an act he referred to as one of 'reconciliation', he issued invitations to a champagne reception to his six main protagonists – those financial journalists and gossip column editors who had vowed to destroy him. Either through curiosity or fear, all invitations were accepted. He went to great lengths to ensure that everything would happen exactly as he wished it to. Strict instructions were given to his secretary; he himself would set the agenda.

His guests would arrive at 7.30pm, be greeted, and shown to the boardroom by his secretary and a smile of waitresses who had been chosen for their beauty above their ability to dispense drinks. The heating in the room would be turned up to 75°F. His secretary and the waitresses had been instructed to keep all wine glasses filled at all times. This would prove no arduous task, as all of those invited were hardened drinkers who had never acquired the habit of refusing a free drink. His secretary and the waitresses had also been instructed to keep his guests happy for at least 90 minutes. The heat in the room would slowly be increased to 85°F. There would be no food.

He was seated behind his curved mahogany desk, when at exactly 9pm they were ushered into his office and to the row of seats that had been deliberately arranged as close to his desk as possible. He had removed his jacket.

All carried champagne flutes with them into the room. Jackie immediately recognised the two women among them. One, he had known briefly – too briefly for her; too long for him. She was tall with fine features, intelligent, but dull-eyed. She was dressed from head to foot in red, her hair a mass of red ringlets better suited to someone younger than she. She wore large, red-rimmed spectacles and even redder lipstick – most of which, he noticed, had been transferred to the rim of her glass and to her teeth. Tottering precariously on too-high red heels, she had a reputation for being permanently drunk, which was unkind. She was only drunk often. Unsurprisingly, and showing little imagination, she insisted she be referred to as 'Red'. Her column was entitled 'Red Alert'.

The other was a mousy woman, cleverer than Red. Smaller, plumper, she had short-cropped black hair and was unable to prevent her large, round, white-rimmed spectacles from resting on the edge of her nose, which fortunately was of sufficient size to take the weight. She was dressed in tight fitting black trousers and a tighter fitting white blouse, with the top three buttons unfastened. For a reason known only to her, she wore a brightly coloured, spangled, Spanish picador's jacket. She spoke a little too deeply for Jackie to show any interest in her and resented the fact that he had told her so.

All the men were sweating profusely, despite having removed their jackets and loosened their ties. They placed their jackets on the back of their seats and sat down, a little nervously. Jackie stood up to address them.

'Ladies and gentlemen of the press, welcome. In view of the little battle we have collectively endured, which thank goodness is now at an end, I think it only fair that I try to answer those questions which have so agitated you for so long, and which precipitated the whole sorry saga. I refer of course, to how I was supposedly,' he emphasised this word supposedly, 'able to choose those shares that seemed instantly to soar in price, whilst others with their fine education, their sophistication, with their contacts and in-depth knowledge of the markets, and with their years of experience, somehow seemed unable to do. Was it true, you wondered? Was it true, you asked, that I could see into the future?'

All listened intently, wine glasses resting on the floor beside them.

'Many of you have stated both publicly and privately that I am a gypsy. Indeed, I am indebted to you for supplying so many humorous sobriquets alluding to this fact.'

To their discomfort, Jackie slowly read out all the names they had applied to him.

'There are others, of course,' he said, 'but those are rather less pleasant and perhaps shouldn't be repeated in front of ladies.' Both women blushed. They knew that the worst of the sobriquets had been written by them.

There was a ripple of nervous laughter. No-one spoke.

'If indeed I were a gypsy, I would simply have done what any self-respecting gypsy would do. First, I would remove the sparkly red velvet cover from my crystal ball and peer into it to see if the answer lay there. Sometimes, most unusually, it did not. If that proved the case, then I would resort to the method employed by my forebears for thousands of years; one that never failed.' Jackie's voice was low; he was quite calm. He smiled his widest smile.

'This is that method.' He leaned forward and swept everything off his desk. Telephones, inkwell, writing pad, pens, pencils, ornaments, and his wine glass were sent crashing onto the wooden floor. Everyone gasped in astonishment and sat bolt upright.

Reaching down to the side of the desk, he removed a large cloth that was covering a small, square, wire cage. He reached into the cage, and in one swift, upward arching movement, swung a live cockerel, which he had gripped firmly by the neck, and crashed it down onto his desk. Brown and white feathers flew into the air as the cockerel kicked and struggled. Its terrified eyes seemed to pop from its head, but no sound emerged from its gaping beak. Its bright red cockscomb shone against Jackie's white shirt sleeve.

He held it down with one hand, and with the other opened a drawer in his desk. He pulled out a large, silver bladed axe, held it for a second over the bird, stared down at his appalled audience, then brought the axe down with a crash, severing the bird's head from its body. The axe lay embedded in the desk, quivering. Blood spurted out over Jackie's shirt and over those closest to the cockerel – the two women, who screamed in unison.

The men reacted as if they had been poleaxed. But Jackie was not finished. He pushed the severed head forward until it hung over the front of his desk, its cockscomb drooping over the edge. Then he reached back into the desk and withdrew a short, thin, stainless-steel knife. He plunged the knife into the cockerel's neck where the breastplates joined, cutting down until they were sufficiently loosened for him to snap them apart with his fingers. He forced them open to reveal the bird's innards. He scooped out the still steaming, tiny red and yellow heart, lungs, and liver, then the remaining entrails, allowing them to fall over and between his blood-soaked fingers, seemingly studying them intently.

By now his audience was in a state of panic. The lack of food, the surfeit of champagne, the too-hot room, all combined to create the effect Jackie had planned. Red had fainted and fallen into the space between her seat and the front of the desk. There was insufficient room to accommodate her, causing her to collapse into a little heap on her knees, one side of her face pressed hard against the desk, the severed cockscomb head staring down at her.

The men were quietly groaning, some being sick into their cupped hands, others with their heads between their knees breathing deeply. Jackie surveyed the human wreckage with satisfaction.

Lifting the entrails, he let them fall slowly through his fingers. 'Here, ladies and gentlemen of the press, is the answer. Now you know how to see into the future.'

The woman in the white blouse was weeping into a blood-speckled handkerchief. Red was being helped to her feet by a fat man with vomit down the front of his shirt – Red's vomit. The bedlam gave way to childlike whimpering as each leaned on each other for support. They made their way to the door.

At a nod from Jackie, his secretary, who had witnessed the proceedings, unlocked it. They filed out past her like war-weary refugees. When they had left, Jackie said to her, 'Have this lot cleaned up,' and left.

CHAPTER NINETEEN

It was a Saturday in December, and he had to make one of his infrequent visits to the nearby seaside town. It was a tired town of once-imposing Victorian buildings built of stone on high hills and in low valleys that sloped down through pine woods to the sea and the once proud but now decaying pier. The high-minded Victorians who had built the town had laid out wide squares and ornamental parks with bandstands and boating lakes for the recreation of the townspeople. A railway station of great grandeur opened the town to the outside world, and hotels sprang up to welcome the incomers. For many years, the town and its citizens prospered.

The newly-enriched built palatial homes on the high cliffs overlooking the sea, and the clement climate allowed them to stock their gardens and glass houses with expensive fauna and stately palms. The long stretches of golden sand, the clean air, and temperate waters, attracted the health conscious and newly retired. The town centre became home to fashionable departmental stores and businesses of every conceivable nature. The secular gave a little ground to the spiritual, which allowed a small number of uninspiring churches of competing denominations to settle quietly behind high spiked, iron railings, where they lay hidden among the shadows of their more illustrious neighbours.

These once great buildings had long ago surrendered to the ravages of the east wind and the salt air. The shops, like elderly courtesans, did their best to disguise their faults, but exposed to the cold, cruel light of a December morning, they deceived no-one, and no amount of Christmas baubles could distract from their shabby façades.

Jackie had to fight his way through crowds of Christmas shoppers in their heavy, dull winter clothes, with their heavy, dull expressions, in order to reach his office. The pavements were infested with those calling themselves God's Soldiers, in their red and black military uniforms, who sucked in the crisp, cold air and exhaled into their highly polished brass instruments. Songs of the season filled the air, and a pretty young female soldier shook a tambourine with one hand and held out a small, wicker basket with the other. Those who gave were wished a Happy Christmas; those who did not, were not.

Buskers played with renewed vigour, confident that their lack of talent would be overlooked at this time of the year, stray dogs – unaware of the season – barked and howled in protest. In the doorways of long abandoned shops, beggars dusted off their most soulful expressions, those specially reserved for this, their busy season, before sitting cross-legged on the hard, cold, stone floor. In front of them a battered flat cap; at its side, childlike scribble on a piece of cardboard, advised prospective donors of the number of children they had sired, all of whom were starving and shoeless. Densely packed crowds of strained-faced shoppers, hands tightly gripping their purchases, streamed in and out of the shops in a barely controlled frenzy of un-choreographed dance. All the colours of Christmas could not dispel the deep gloom that enveloped him. It was with undisguised relief he arrived at his office and normality.

The crowds were no less dense when, business completed, he once again found himself among them. Dusk was descending, and the coloured lights that were stretched between the lampposts swung alarmingly in the snow-littered wind. Struggling through the throng to his car, he hardly noticed the young man handing out leaflets to the passers-by, most of whom refused his offer. Those that reluctantly accepted them, as a matter of good manners, glanced at the content before dropping them into the gutter.

Jackie glumly accepted one and thrust it into his pocket. Safely returned to his car, he took it out and studied it. It was, he read, an invitation to a service celebrating the third advent of Christmas, the following day. Jackie was curious. He had never been to such a service. In fact, he had never been inside a church. He recalled with bitterness how as a boy, walking the streets seeking shelter, it had been apparent to him that all church doors were bolted.

However, having nothing better to do – Sundays being the most dispiriting of days – he decided to investigate further.

And so it came to pass.

The old Priory was a few miles from the town centre and prided itself that people had prayed within its walls for a thousand years. He parked his car nearby and walked through the wooden gateway and along the yew-lined path that led to the Priory entrance. Once inside, he was met by a matronly woman who greeted him with an insincere smile, a songbook, and a leaflet on which the order of service was listed. He was directed towards a cavernous space and made the long journey down the central aisle between an ocean of empty seats. He reflected that he should have brought sandwiches and a flask of tea to sustain him on this long pilgrimage.

Despite the solemnity of the occasion and the advertising campaign, the Priory was thinly sown with worshippers. He sat down a few rows behind an elderly male couple – father and son perhaps – who he concluded would know the correct procedure. The congregation swelled to fifteen – mainly couples and elderly. The choirmaster, in his best-pressed suit, quietly led in the be-smocked, songbook-nursing choirboys, who quickly settled themselves into their seats and into their routine. Songs were sung.

The preacher approached his flock with the beatific expression of a martyr who could feel the flames licking at his feet. He mounted the spiral stone stairs that led up to the lectern and began to talk down to the upturned faces. He spoke not in the parables that Jackie had expected, but in simple homilies. Reading between the well-practised lines of his sermon, Jackie quickly detected the whiff of politics.

A new priest – a new young priest, whose name he was not prepared to divulge – had been chosen to lead the parish, intoned the elderly priest through a smile of gritted teeth. He then commenced to lecture the unfortunate unnamed priest in his absence with all of the dangers associated with change. The congregation, who had long ago learned the art of listening without hearing, appeared uninterested in both the lecture and the lecturer. Sensing no rioting in the offing, he changed tack, heaping praise upon the young man and his superiors in their foresightedness.

The choir was called upon to sing, and sang. Orders were read out, prayers were offered up by the priest and answered by the little congregation, Jackie bobbing up and down in unison with them. As the choir rose to sing the service to its close, a simple looking boy – *possibly chosen for security reasons*, Jackie ventured to himself – was entrusted to pass round the pewter collection plate. Jackie, following the example of the others, dropped a few coins in but remained unconvinced that he had received value for money.

The service over, he made to leave. At the exit, the priest shook his hand and coldly wished him, 'Good morning', moving on quickly to someone he had recognised and hoped he had impressed. Left alone, Jackie noticed that the high walls in the entrance that led into the main body of the Priory were decorated with ancient wooden plaques and stone engravings of those who, through the ages, had made good at the expense of others, and at the behest of the priest had given up some of their land and most of their money to the Priory in exchange for a promise of a smooth passage to heaven.

Jackie, his cynicism only enhanced by his visit, let his imagination run riot. God, the God-fearing people had been assured by their priest, was like no other.

He was to be in awe of.

To be held in high esteem.

To wonder at, to fear.

To be on the right side of.

God, their priest assured them, was not someone to be crossed.

Jackie left the church, and with no-one to prevent him from doing so, closed the high, arched, wooden doors behind him.

CHAPTER TWENTY

In preparation for his planned departure, he had already decided to split his business empire, for that was what it had become, into four separate divisions. The manager of each of these divisions would submit a monthly report to him via Donald Simpson. Only he would know where to forward them. Every three months, each division manager would carry out a full and confidential report on one of the other divisions. Again, they would be forwarded to him via Donald.

Donald Simpson, Josiah Abneth his accountant, and his private secretary Mrs Kanning, would oversee all the businesses and collectively submit a report to him every six months. Jackie had told them he was taking a long holiday. All openly approved and applauded his decision, but secretly all were apprehensive. After all, Jackie *was* the business, and all were fearful what might happen in his absence.

Jackie also told them that he would reappear often, without notice, which both comforted and alarmed them. All of them – the four division managers, the accountant, and Mrs Kanning – Jackie had met secretly, and confided to each that they alone would be required to send him a secret report on any and all aspects of the business, to an address that only they would have. Thrilled and proud to be entrusted with this covert task, each in turn vowed their allegiance to him.

It was exactly seven days after his visit to the Priory, and he had one final act to perform. An act that he hoped would bring the matter to its conclusion.

It promised to be a lovely, late December Sunday morning. Darkness was surrendering to a watercolour sunrise. A light frost lit the lawns and the grey, Welsh slate roof tiles. Berries glowed in the hedgerows. The skeletal frames of lime and ash, stripped of their leaves by the easterly wind, were pressed against the skyline like thumb prints. Too early yet for the church bells to peal, the whirr of the milk floats – their bottles shivering in their crates – was the only sound to be heard. Until the stillness was shattered by the harsh rat-a-tat-tat of door knockers, causing the songbirds to flee their roosts with a great beating of wings, and rise above and swoop over the glistening rooftops.

A short while later, in various locations across the city and across suburbia, four wives and two husbands, hunched over their breakfast tables, having been raised too soon from their gentle slumbers, sat in stunned silence, head in hands, as they desperately sought to hold back the tears filling their eyes. Again and again, they studied the contents of the large brown envelopes that had been handed to them.

Jackie professed no knowledge of the workings of men's minds, so had no way of knowing how the two husbands would react to the exposing of their wives' infidelities. He did, however, have knowledge of the way women's minds worked. *Fortunate*, he thought, *would be those whose relationship would be speedily terminated.* The remainder would face a future of subtle torture. Torture that would increase as the husband grew older and frailer. Women, Jackie knew, did not forgive, did not forget. They simply waited.

The clown arrived at exactly 2.30pm at the hotel where Lord and Lady Eaton were celebrating, with their children and grandchildren, the fifteenth birthday of their favourite grandson, Toby. Everyone smiled as the clown entered awkwardly, amusingly, through the revolving doors. He bowed to all who greeted him, squirting water from the flower in his lapel as he did so. He wore his outrageous clown's costume with aplomb, the wide lapel chequered jacket, the baggy trousers held up by loose braces, the flowery shirt, the too tall top hat. He carried a string of coloured balloons in one hand and a pail of confetti water in the other which, appearing to stumble, he deposited over the heads of the hotel guests, who shrieked with laughter. The faces of everyone around him glowed with pleasure.

Everyone loved a clown.

His make-up was perfect – the big, bright red nose, the wide chalk-white smile, the reddened lips, the rouged cheeks, were all clown perfect.

However, anyone who looked closer would see that this clown did not have the laughter-filled eyes of a clown; this clown's eyes seemed to leap out from his face – hypnotic, black, cruel, dead. He plodded into the dining room.

The pianist, believing him to be part of Toby's birthday celebrations, began playing 'Happy Birthday'. Everyone, diners and waiters alike, began singing and applauding. The birthday party looked at each other in bewilderment, wondering which one of them had arranged this treat. Toby looked embarrassed.

To their delight, the clown threw the last of the confetti water over a table of diners and put down his pail. He reached into his baggy trousers and withdrew a large, black folder which had hung around his waist. He took out a large sheaf of documents and dozens of black and white photographs. As he walked between the tables towards where Lord Eaton's family were seated, he threw them one by one into the air, the laughing and applauding diners reaching up to catch them as they fell.

The clown stood directly in front of Lord Eaton's table. Slowly and deliberately, he began dealing the photographs to each member of Lord Eaton's family in turn, as a croupier might deal out a deck of cards to a group of gamblers. The final most explicit photograph he dealt to Toby. As the documents and photographs were retrieved and studied, the laughter died. The children on Lord Eaton's table began to cry.

Jackie smiled as he turned away. The matter had been settled to his satisfaction.

CHAPTER TWENTY-ONE

He had won this fight, but there would be others. There would always be others – real, imagined, or contrived. He had achieved satisfaction of a sort but not the expected euphoria he felt such a victory merited. There was no towering triumph, only hollowness inside. Only a pit-of-the-stomach sickness and an all-consuming weariness he had never before experienced.

And one more face to haunt his dreams, that of the boy Toby.

Melancholy took a hold.

Doubt took hold.

What if he had been wrong, that this so-called ancestral blood that drove him along and his gift for prophecy had been nothing but a delusion.

Was he prophetic? Did the numbers really protect him, or were they there simply to nourish the belief in his destiny without adding anything of substance to that belief? Even in his boyhood had that unflinching belief been nothing more than a hanging onto a hope, a blindness to the reality of what his life was – a longed for escape. His grandmother had provided that escape, and he had willingly submitted to her will, convincing himself that this was his destiny while she convinced herself it would be he who would carry that ancient bloodline forward.

Could he believe in anything any more?

Could he believe in anything his grandmother had said or taught?

Had she seen in him her own image, and gloried in that countenance? Had she deceived him? In her longing to bequeath something, anything, had she instead ensured that his only inheritance would be one of hatred? He was the monster that she had delighted in creating, and had set free to brutalise and destroy all that came into contact with him. And he had happily colluded in its creation. He might have had no choice of the road he was set down on by his parents, or of the vehicle on that road provided by his grandmother, but it had been his choice not to change direction or call a halt to that journey.

Was he destined to become what he had become, or had her teachings, her hatred of weaknesses, her detestation of everybody and anything, especially love, cauterised his true nature? Had that tiny spark of goodness first discovered by his adored Miss Lucy, and breathed into flame by Suzanne, never been fully extinguished?

And now, if he was to find any contentment or love in his new life, he must first re-examine his old life and reject all that had gone before.

He must unlearn. *He must unlearn.*

It was time for him to leave.

As he was packing his suitcase, he heard the closing stages of the nine o'clock news. It announced that 'due to a sudden deterioration in his health, Lord Eaton had resigned as head of the newspaper group he had founded, and would be returning to his native South Africa'.

As Jackie sat in the taxi taking him to the boat train, a furious hailstorm beat against the roof of the car.

To be continued with:-
RETURN TO EDEN:
The Wonderfilled Years

CPSIA information can be obtained
at www.ICGtesting.com
Printed in the USA
LVHW080750190422
716542LV00003B/90/J

9 781839 759208